HAMMERED

PIPPA GRANT

LILI VALENTE

Michaela.
Never be afraid to
be you. :)

Pippa Grant
♡

ABOUT HAMMERED

Hammered

A Bad Boy / Good Girl / Forbidden Romance Romantic Comedy

I didn't mean to kidnap the groom.

It was an accident.

Mostly...

At least I didn't take much time to plan it. It was more of a spur of the moment kidnapping. Does that count?

One minute, the town's bad boy is standing at the altar about to marry the world's most evil kindergarten teacher. The next, he's passed out in my Vespa sidecar with his bride hot on our tail.

But I didn't have a choice! I couldn't stand by and watch

Jace O'Dell be blackmailed into a loveless marriage. And besides, what's a little kidnapping between friends?

Okay, so maybe we're not just friends...

And maybe I can't quit thinking about that night at his bar when he closed up early and had *me* on the rocks.

And maybe this crazy stunt is going to blow up in both of our faces.

If it does, I'm blaming the moonshine.

Even though the only thing I'm hammered on when it comes to Jace is love—straight up, no chaser.

ONE

Jace O'Dell
(aka a man who only *thinks* he's on the verge of leaving his past behind)

Nothing goes better with tequila than a moonbeam. An Olivia Moonbeam, to be specific.

Or so I assume.

I've never actually had Olivia, though I've dreamed about it for what feels like forever.

And I'll go right on dreaming, because moonbeams and rough-around-the-edges bartenders go together like champagne and a crap sandwich. Olivia is so high above me, we're barely the same species, but even if we were, tonight's not the night to make a play for a girl who's out of my league.

Not with everything Olivia's been through in the past twenty-four hours.

So I'm standing here, wiping the same burn mark on the

bar that I know will never come clean, ignoring a half-empty tequila bottle that promises to make me forget why I don't deserve moonbeams if I'll only give in and have another shot.

But I won't.

Because I want to remember every minute with her, and one more shot of tequila will take me past pleasantly buzzed and all the way to hammered.

"One more, please. Something stronger this time," Olivia says, pushing her glass back across the bar. "My sorrows don't feel drowned yet. Shouldn't they be drowned by now, Jace?"

God, just hearing my name on her lips makes my blood pump faster. I've been one degree of hung up on her or another since she landed here in Happy Cat exactly six break-ups ago.

Not her break-ups.

My break-ups. With the same woman. Because Ginger and I are stuck on an on-again-off-again merry-go-round-from-hell relationship that's driving me out of my damned mind.

Hence, the tequila, even though Ginger and I are *off* right now and I rarely drink while I'm behind the bar.

I'm a professional, dammit, and I take my job seriously.

Which is why this usually happy little lightweight across from me is getting the weakest Smoky-Pepper in history.

I top off Olivia's ice and fill in the cracks with Dr Pepper and the tiniest drop of whiskey. But she doesn't notice I've skimped on the good stuff. Poor thing's a wreck. She's unraveled the braids she was wearing when she got here, and now her blond hair's a hot, crinkled mess.

A fucking adorable mess.

"Wasn't your fault, Liv," I say, passing the glass back to her.

"But I almost committed *murder*."

I shrug. "I almost committed murder once."

Her eyes go even wider. "*No.*"

Grinning's not my thing, but hell, what do I have to lose by flirting with her? And there's no one else around this late to tell her that it wasn't her fault a woman had an allergic reaction to the sno-cones she was serving at the farmer's market tonight. And somebody definitely needs to comfort her.

It should be someone better than me. But she's here. And I'm here.

So I lean onto the bar at her level and I grin. "You know that giant bunny they put out in Sunshine Square for Easter every year?"

"I love that bunny!" She claps her hands and bounces, which makes *everything* bounce, but I'm not ogling, I swear. If this is ogling, I also ogle her personality and her shoes, because she has the weirdest shoes. But I like them. All of them.

"I almost murdered it," I whisper conspiratorially.

She snort-laughs into her glass like she's drunk on Dr Pepper, which is also adorable. Who gets drunk on Dr Pepper?

Olivia Moonbeam, that's who.

"Gluing the pink fur on it was my punishment for welding the principal's car doors shut," I explain. "Got so much of it stuck to myself, I was pink up to my elbows for a week."

She snort-laughs into her glass again, a sound like a baby pig squeaking in joy.

I think. I don't know any baby pigs, personally, but they're cute. And she's cute, so cute I can't look away from her blue eyes as she whispers, "I switched the liquid foundation in my mom's makeup case for green paint, and she did an entire zombie movie before she realized it. But the paint started flaking off in the middle of filming and a guy broke out in a rash that made the boom operator think we had a for real zombie outbreak on our hands, so he quit." Her eyes scrunch up and her chin wobbles, and *shit*, I think she's going to cry. "But I was just trying to help. Mom was afraid there wouldn't be enough foundation, but I knew there'd be enough paint."

"You helped," I assure her. "You helped that boom guy realize he had a seriously overactive imagination. I'll bet he went out and got a normal job, with no zombies in it, and lived happily ever after."

Her lips part, and she lifts those Blue Lace Agate-colored eyes to mine like I'm some kind of hero. I know they're Blue Lace Agate blue, because it's the first thing she said to me all those break-ups ago. *Hi, I'm Olivia Moonbeam, and I have Blue Lace Agate-colored eyes. It's the best gemstone for chasing away fear. So if you're ever afraid, you can just look in my eyes. I sense you're afraid right now, and that's okay. Losing someone we love is one of the scariest things there is.*

I had no clue how she knew what I was afraid of that day—I don't make a habit of talking to strangers, or anyone else, about my feelings.

But she was right, losing love *is* scary, even if it's love that isn't in such good shape anymore, love that probably should have been laid to rest many moons ago.

But maybe it's time to stop being afraid. Maybe I should look into Olivia's eyes and stop worrying that I'll never be quite good enough, or worthy of being someone's hero.

"You're a very good bartender," she says in a reverent whisper. "You always know what to say to make people feel better."

I don't know shit about helping people—I just get them too buzzed to care about their problems for a while—but the tequila's humming in my blood and whispering those words that usually get me in trouble.

She likes you. Go for it. You can make each other feel good, at least for a night.

But Olivia and trouble don't go together. Olivia and accidents, yes. Olivia and new-age mumbo-jumbo, yes. Olivia and absolute fucking sweetness so pure you can tell there's nothing but goodness in her, right down to her marrow, no doubt in my mind.

Olivia and trouble? Never.

But maybe things can change. Maybe *I* can change.

And maybe this breakup with Ginger is finally the last one.

For once, the thought tastes more like relief than failure, making my voice lighter as I motion behind the bar. "You want a grand tour of where the magic happens?"

Olivia's eyes widen and her lips spread in a smile, like I've just offered her a new car. She bounces on her stool again. "When's your birthday?"

"My—what?"

"Your birthday!"

"December 16."

"I *knew* it!"

"Well, you came to my party last year, right? Thought I saw you there." I *know* I saw her there, and I remember every time I almost, but didn't, swing her way while she was standing beneath the mistletoe.

"Oh, right." She stops, blushing as she adds with a loose shake of her head, "So that's how I knew. Doesn't matter. What matters is that I did your star chart earlier, and you won't believe—" She flutters her fingers, knocking her glass over. We both lunge for it and our hands connect, hers slender and smooth, mine thick and notched from years of working on cars without gloves and carving shit while I'm buzzed and getting into other kinds of trouble.

"Sorry," she sighs, eyes shining again. "I'm a disaster."

I grab a rag and sweep everything—ice, soda, the glass, everything—straight into the trash, and then I latch onto her chin until she lifts those gorgeous Blue Lace Agates. "You're the brightest spot in this town. *Not* a disaster."

"Really?" She blinks.

"Really and truly."

"That's...so nice of you to say." A goofy grin spreads over her face, and if she hadn't been sitting here nursing the weakest whiskey drinks in existence for the past three hours, I'd swear she was tipsy.

Hell, I think *I'm* tipsy. Even though I've been sticking to Dr Pepper for the past hour.

"No, *you're* nice," I say, my voice soft and rough at the same time. "And so beautiful...inside and out."

Those pretty eyes widen, and then she's pushing up off her stool, grabbing my face and pressing her mouth to mine. The next thing I know, we're making out hot and heavy behind my bar, rolling on the floor, knocking into the dishwasher, the racks of glasses, our legs tangling in the hoses for the taps.

And then, fuck...our clothes are coming off. They shouldn't be coming off, but it feels so good. To touch her, to taste her skin, to hear the sexy sounds she makes as I bare one beautiful part of her after another.

"Do you have freckles? I have freckles on my chest in the shape of Orion. See?" With one smooth move of her long, slender arms, she tugs her ruffly tee shirt over her head. But the fabric gets caught in the bangles around her wrists, and I sit there on the floor beside her, momentarily stupefied that Olivia Moonbeam is seducing me with freckle constellations.

She hiccups, giggles, and finally pulls her arms free, her bracelets sliding to her elbows, and then back down to her wrists. Her bra is blue lace, and I don't know why, but I sort of expected her bras to be made of cotton candy, though I like the lace just as much. "See? Here?" She touches seven freckles dotting the top of her right breast.

"Olivia?" I rasp out.

"Yes?" She smiles, all soft and warm, and for a minute, I wonder if she knows who she's showing her constellation to, and then I grin, because I've never had a woman show me her constellation before.

"You're not drunk, are you?" I ask, though I seriously can't imagine how she could have gotten sauced on the less-than-full-shot of whiskey I dribbled into the three drinks she's had tonight.

She shakes her head. "No. Are you? I saw you sneaking a shot. You looked sad."

"I was sad," I tell her. "But I'm not anymore."

Her smile spreads wider, and yeah, those eyes are taking away all of my fears.

"We're a lot alike," she tells me.

I burst out laughing, which takes me by surprise, because I don't usually laugh when I'm with a woman. Probably because of the woman I'm with. Ginger and I are usually too busy rehashing the same old shit to spend much time laughing together anymore.

But Olivia—she's pure, innocent, sunshiny California, the kind of person who makes you feel like it's always okay to laugh. Although, with the way she's straddling me, nestling the seam of her tiny cut-off shorts against my hard-on, I'm starting to rethink the *innocent* part, a fact that only makes her more irresistible.

"Can I—" She pauses to hiccup, then dissolves into giggles, and I laugh along with her, because *fuck*, she's so cute and refreshing and sexy as hell with her twinkling eyes and the way she's putting the *bedroom* into her bedroom hair.

"Can I tell you something?" she rushes out.

"Only if you promise not to tell," I murmur, and then we're both laughing again, because that didn't make any sense, and *shit*, I did only have one shot of tequila, didn't I?

"I like you," she announces around another hiccup.

I don't deserve that, but I don't have the willpower to tell her so. Especially when she loops her arms around my bare back again and starts swaying in my lap to some music only she can hear, but that's making my cock ache with a desperate need to know if hiccups make her pussy clench.

"I like you, too," I murmur instead, dropping my head to her chest and licking a path over Orion. And soon she's panting, moaning my name even though she's still in those short shorts, and my hands are down exploring every inch of her long, smooth legs instead of diving between them.

This is a bad idea.

But I can't remember why.

Especially when she locks her lips on mine again, and I taste sweet Dr Pepper and heady *Olivia*. She's an all natural, organic, free-range nymph who tastes like rainbows and spring rain, and I can't resist her. Can't stop touching her, exploring her gorgeous body.

Soon we're rolling again, both of us tugging off our shorts, helping each other. We slam into the cabinets, and an errant roll of paper towels falls on my head, reminding me to grab a condom.

I don't know why it reminds me, but it does, making me snort-chuckle, which makes her giggle, and then hiccup, and *damn*, have I ever laughed while I kissed a woman?

"Jace," she whispers, her eyes locking on mine. "I want you so much, but I don't want to take advantage of you."

I blink at her once, then twice, and then I'm snort-laughing again. "Willing participant, Sunshine. So very willing."

Her whole body lights up when she smiles. "So you feel it too," she says happily, and I don't think, I don't question, I just *nod*, because maybe I *can* deserve her.

I've liked Olivia Moonbeam since the moment she walked into my bar asking for organic cranberry juice with a shot of lime. So maybe, just maybe, I can be worthy of this kind, flirty, joyful woman. Put my past behind me.

Start a new chapter. A new fucking book.

Every day's an opportunity to wake up to the miracle of being present in your own life! Olivia's always saying.

Today's my chance for a miracle.

I slide into her as she arches into me, and she hiccups, her pussy squeezing my cock as she giggles, and it's heaven.

Her hands roaming my skin.

Her tongue tangling with mine.

Her slick heat squeezing me with every thrust and every hiccup and every laugh, and when her breath goes shallow and her hips strain hard against my pelvis, I flick my thumb over her clit—*god*, I want to taste her everywhere and do this every night, here, in the square, in my bed, on my motorcycle, *everywhere*—and she clamps hard around me, crying my name, carrying me with her. I lose all control, coming so hard I'm amazed the condom doesn't shoot off my dick.

Holy fuck.

I laugh-groan into the crook of her neck while I'm still coming, and she replies with a giggle-sigh of pure happiness, and I'm still buried deep inside her and twitching and oversensitive and jumping with every hiccup that squeezes my cock, and *this*…

This is what I've been waiting for my entire life.

Olivia.

Peace.

Goodness.

Laughter.

"I'm gonna fucking deserve you," I promise. "Deserve this."

"You already do deserve it," she says. "We're all just *people*, Jace. Doing our *people* thing. And sometimes we get it right, and sometimes we get it wrong, but we all have hearts and dreams and we all deserve joy. Pleasure." She smiles. "And when souls connect, they connect. Sometimes you don't have to try so hard."

I'm punching the next person who calls her a ditz. Right in the face. She's so smart and sweet and sexy as hell.

She squirms beneath me, grinning as she asks, "Walk me home?" Her hair's a kinky mess, her lip gloss is smeared over her cheek, and she's half-in, half-out of her bra, but even if she stays just like this I'll be walking home the most beautiful woman I've ever met.

"Yeah," I say. "Yeah, I wanna walk you home."

She grins.

I grin back.

And then I kiss her again.

Because this moment?

This is my moment to finally start my life *right*.

TWO

Jace

Nothing can make this night anything but perfect. I'm sure of it. And then Olivia and I step out the back door into the humid night, and come face to face with a fat ass raccoon with an attitude.

"George," I hiss, "get out of there."

My brother's pet trash panda, George Cooney, lifts a slicked-up head from the garbage can next door. He got into some lube earlier—don't ask—and now he's apparently out for a midnight snack.

"Oh my god, I forgot I almost killed someone," Olivia gasps.

George rolls his eyes and dives back into the trash, coming up with a red ball stuck on his nose, making him look like he's a clown refugee from the abandoned circus school a couple of blocks away.

After making sure the back door of the bar is locked, I

pocket my keys and tuck Olivia's hand into mine. "No, you didn't. George. Go on. Go home before someone sees you and calls animal control."

She gasps. "They wouldn't!"

They probably wouldn't. But George doesn't know that.

Probably.

Maybe.

I can't tell if George is an evil genius or just exceptionally spoiled by my big brother, but he exudes a weird confidence that makes you think he's got it all figured the fuck out.

Even when he's wearing a clown nose.

Ignoring me, George dives back into the garbage can and tosses out a squirrel wearing a coat.

Wait, *what*?

Olivia gasps again as the thing rolls to a stop in front of us, and I toe the…*gentleman squirrel*?…to one side.

"Don't kick it!" she screeches.

"Don't worry. It's dead." I think. Yes, another gentle prod of my boot proves it's definitely dead.

And definitely a squirrel.

Wearing a trench coat. And a plaid vest. And a…moustache?

"Oh, you poor thing!" Before I can stop her, Olivia's bent over and picked it up. "What have they *done* to you?"

Aw, hell. "Looks like one of Gordon's Mighty Squirrels."

She gasps again. "But…but…he had a long life ahead of him. And now he's not only stuffed, but someone threw him away. And *he's carrying a pipe*. His lungs are doomed even in *death*."

I pat her shoulder. Then I hug her closer, because she feels so good, and she smells like sex, and she's still hiccupping, and now I'm smiling again. "I'm betting he died of natural causes after a long happy life. And the pipe is just for decoration."

Her brow furrows. "Still. He shouldn't be setting a bad example for the other squirrels. Or for you, George Cooney. Don't smoke, not even a pipe. All tobacco is dangerous tobacco. And if your mouth smells like an ashtray, none of the lady raccoons will want you, and that would be a shame for a handsome fella like you."

He eyeballs her, still wearing that clown nose, and I snort at his ridiculousness. What other animal could look down on a guy while wearing a clown nose?

Only George.

Crazy trash panda.

I tug her hand. "C'mon. You have work in the morning."

"No, I have to work when my aura starts manifesting productive energy, which might happen in the morning, but our work culture is flexible"—she pauses to hiccup, then smiles shyly at me—"and body rhythms sometimes change."

My body's rhythm is suddenly gearing up for another dance.

I pick a stray peanut out of her hair and vow that next time, I'm treating her like a lady.

Bedroom.

Candles.

Champagne.

Whatever rocks she keeps that are supposed to be good for orgasms.

Some of that scented stuff too.

"George?" Olivia tilts her head at him. "Is he...?"

"Drunk? Probably." I sigh as the raccoon falls off the trash cans, knocking his fake red nose loose. And then I grin. Again. I don't know who I am, grinning this much, but it's growing on me. "He goes through the recycling, drinks the dregs out of all the beer bottles." I crouch down, getting on the tipsy bastard's level. "George. C'mon. Up we go, buddy. Home is this way."

He blinks at me, then lumbers to his feet, swaying sideways as he shoves the remains of a soft pretzel into his mouth like a cigar, clearly not taking Olivia's lecture on smoking to heart.

"Whose trash cans are those?" she demands, cradling the squirrel in one arm like the world's weirdest looking baby.

"Used to be for the Happy Cat Treasures store next door before it closed, but now they're pretty much first come, first served. The guys back there dump stuff here sometimes on their way out of town." I point to the row of small houses, mostly rental properties the bank snapped up in the recession, behind the bar. "George. Popcorn? You want popcorn? I bet your dad will make you some if you get your ass home."

Even drunk, the trash panda knows the magic word. He waddles his plump butt around and heads in the right direction. We follow, because Olivia's house is this way too, and because George is listing worse than my baby brother, Clint, the night we got him wasted to celebrate his homecoming from his last deployment.

I miss Clint. He's a Marine, stationed in Japan right now, and we don't see him often enough.

By the time we hit the town square a couple blocks away, Olivia's named the taxidermied squirrel Sir Pendleton Macavoy, Investigator at Large, and fluffed his tail back into its original shape. George is ambling a little straighter. And I'm feeling lighter with every step.

Impulsively, I turn, grab Olivia by the waist, and kiss her hard. She's the Right in a world that's always felt a little bit Wrong, and I don't want to stop kissing her. Ever. Especially when she loops her arms around my shoulders, kissing me back, while the squirrel's tail tickles my neck.

We stumble through the square like that, kissing and holding onto each other, her giggling, me grinning, until I bang my shoe on something metal and a weird huff-squeak sound fills the air.

I pull back before I take Olivia down with me, muttering, "Shit," because that hurt. The huffing sound comes again in response, from the general direction of whatever I just kicked.

What the *fuck* is going on in Happy Cat tonight?

I squat down, ignoring the pain in my foot, and pull out my phone to use the flashlight to check out what's in my path.

A hedgehog in a cage—the metal thing that got my toe —shrinks back in the glare.

"Awww!" Olivia says. "He's so *cute*."

I shine the light on the paper taped to the front of the cage. "I ate too many grapes and shit all over my boyfriend. Free to a good home."

"Well, who fed her too many grapes?" Olivia asks indignantly. She hiccups again and shoves the squirrel at me. "Please hold Sir Pendleton. He doesn't like to be alone."

"I—yeah. Wait. What are you doing?"

"Taking this pumpkin home too. It's a night for finding lost things. I've had these before."

Lost things… Like me.

The thought shuts me up and I keep my peace as she opens the door to the cage, reaching for the hedgehog, who curls away, making me think the little critter's probably not rabid. "What's your name, sweet thing? Why did someone leave you out here?"

George looks back at both of us, then at the sidewalk

leading through the middle of the square, where he was rolling in lube earlier tonight.

Yeah, lube. Olivia works at her best friend's sex toy factory a few blocks away. It's a source of contention around town, but no one can deny that it's bringing in jobs and filling up the rental houses. And making Happy Cat a much more interesting place to live than it was when I was growing up, that's for damned sure.

Although I doubt the company will be welcome back at the farmer's market again for a while after their free samples went so very wrong earlier tonight.

"Come here, baby," Olivia coos. "Don't be afraid, I won't hurt you."

"I can take her cage home and call the shelter in the morning," I offer.

"Shelter? Oh, no. This is serendipity. I'm taking her home. That's right, we're going to be good friends, aren't we, Princess?" As if understanding her offer of friendship and shelter, the hedgehog scuttles into her palms. Olivia stands, beaming at the creature. "Isn't she adorable?"

The roly-poly thing's barely bigger than my fist, and she's sniffing like mad, her little nose going crazy while she stares at me and the stuffed squirrel in my arms. "I think she's freaked out by Sir Pendleton."

"Well, of course," Olivia says with another giggle. "Who wouldn't be? He's disturbing. But she'll get used to him. And come to love him, like we have."

I snort, lips curving into yet another smile.

She glances up at me. "What? You love him; don't deny it. I can feel it in your energy. Sir Pendleton is going to be a very good new friend to you, just wait and see."

I lean in, pressing a kiss to her forehead. "You're right. Love him. And Princess too."

She smiles. "We should call her that. Princess is an excellent name for a hedgehog."

We finish the walk to Olivia's house with a stuffed squirrel and a hedgehog, trailed by a drunk raccoon, and when I realize George is trying to climb the lamppost—last time he did that, he stayed up there for two days before Ryan could talk his fellow firefighters into helping him get his raccoon down—I realize I can't go inside with Olivia. Like a responsible raccoon uncle, I have to make sure George gets home safe too.

I set her stuffed squirrel on the table inside her door, which she's painted with flowers and butterflies that make me smile, and I kiss her goodnight.

Hard.

And deep.

And promising.

"Can I call you tomorrow?" I ask.

"You can call me anytime," she replies.

I leave her house with a spring in my step.

Goodbye, bad boy Jace.

Hello, man who's finally on the right track.

For five minutes anyway.

Until George and I both pause to take a leak behind a trash can a block from Ryan's house and I get fucking arrested because the law enforcement in this town have it in for me.

And then I wake up the next morning to my oldest brother bailing me out of jail, and head home to find Ginger, my ex-girlfriend, waiting on me, saying she misses me, that she wasn't flirting with that out-of-town asshole at my bar last month when I called things off again, and oh, by the way—*she's pregnant with my baby.*

Pregnant, just when I'd finally decided to break free from our toxic bullshit.

It's proof positive that one night with a moonbeam won't change who I am.

I call Olivia to tell her why I have to get back with Ginger, but I feel like a total asshole the entire time, so I make it as short as I can.

She seems sad, but I know she'll move on and be okay. She's better off without a fuck-up like me in her life. I don't deserve her. I've got a rap sheet as long as my arm and more baggage than I can bear to weigh her down with.

I can run from my reputation, but I can't change who I am. As Olivia would say, this is my karma.

And it's time I step up and own it.

THREE

Olivia Moonbeam
(aka an orphan who's really good at saving lost things, but
is still kind of hoping for someone to save her too)

Two weeks later…

I HATE LEAVING Princess von Spooksalot—so named for her tendency to roll into a ball when startled—alone. But if I take her with me to community service, someone at the pet shelter will think she's up for adoption.

Or possibly that she needs therapy. Or that I'm an unfit pet mother due to her love for humping random objects and getting freaked out by almost everything.

So instead, I compromise and call my friend Cassie to ask if she'll hedgehog-sit for me. And since Cassie happens to be watching George Cooney, while her boyfriend, Ryan, is working at the firehouse this weekend, she agrees to let our animals have a playdate.

She also doesn't ask questions or raise eyebrows when I show up with an iPod filled with calming music and a bag of amethysts and rose quartz to place strategically around Ryan's house in an attempt to keep Princess calm.

Though she does lay a concerned hand on my arm and ask, "Everything okay?"

"I just miss Savannah," I blurt, because it's easier to hide behind missing her sister and my best friend than to admit that I'm utterly crushed that Jace is back with his ex-girlfriend.

For one magical night, I thought my world was shifting into place, that I'd finally met my Kindred Penis—the true friend with romantic and sexy benefits I've always hoped to find. Then all my dreams were dashed against the rocks of despair when he called to tell me his ex was pregnant and they were going to "make it work for the baby."

Now I'm numb, lost and sad in a way I haven't been since my mom died.

That's why it's not Princess's fault that she's having trouble adjusting to life in my home. That she shredded my favorite reusable shopping bag, ate her way into a bag of dried chickpeas, and keeps leaving them at Sir Pendleton's feet before she humps his tail—vigorously.

It's my fault. I'm emitting too much negative energy.

Cassie pulls me into a soft, warm hug. "Aww, I miss her too. Have you talked to her lately? She's really enjoying her nanny job over in England."

"Good. She deserves all the happiness and sunshine she can find."

Her brow wrinkles. "I'm worried about you. You've seemed down lately."

I touch the kyanite gemstone dangling from the chain my mom gave me. "I'll be okay. It's just the moon phase."

"Well, if Ryan and I can do anything, let us know."

I force a bright smile, because it's what people expect. *There goes Olivia, smiling again like always.*

And Cassie is dating Jace's brother. I can't burden her with my sadness when it would mean asking her to keep such a huge secret. No good can come of *anyone* knowing about the night Jace and I shared.

Not when he's going to have a baby with another woman...

Nope, I'm not going to think about that. Still smiling, I say, "Thanks so much for watching Princess. She'll be good, I swear."

"No worries. We'll have fun." Cassie props a hand on her hip. "Now remind me again how you ended up with community service? I'm sorry, I've missed a lot of gossip lately."

That's what new love will do to a person. I shrug. "It's not a big deal. I just didn't know it was illegal to moon-bathe in Sunshine Square."

"Moon...bathe?"

"It's good for cleansing negative energy." I roll my eyes. "But I only had my top off so I'm still not sure why it was such a big deal."

"You were topless?" she exclaims, her lips curving.

"Well, negative energy can't always escape through your clothes. And I was under so much stress when we thought the factory was going to close." Okay, okay. So I'm lying to Cassie, but I can't tell her the truth, that I was performing a ritual to cleanse my aura of Jace's touch, his kiss, and all the other things we did to each other that night that I'm doing my best not to think about.

She smiles like she wants to pinch my cheeks. "You're

my favorite nut, you know that? Try to have fun with the animals."

"Will do." I pat Princess goodbye and hop on my Vespa to drive out to Happy Cat's animal sanctuary and rescue farm, ten acres of sweetness and snuggles, where creatures of all sizes, shapes, and species are welcome. When I arrive, I ignore Jace's old pickup parked at the far edge of the dirt lot and pull my scooter to a stop between an ancient Cadillac and a hybrid car.

Because of course Jace and I *both* have community service at the shelter, because his star chart indicates he's destined to connect to the earth during the summer solstice, while mine points to a season of bonding with creature spirits, so naturally we've converged here, like a celestial accident waiting to happen.

But it's okay.

I can do this.

I can see him and not be bereft.

Except he's just so *wrong* with Ginger. Their auras are like peanut butter and sardines, swirled in a blender and tossed into a bathtub. And even though my friend from work, Ruthie May, says Ginger's an amazing kindergarten teacher, I just don't care for the woman.

And I don't like not caring for people. I'm a carer. Caring is one of my number one hobbies. But when it comes to the redhead having Jace's baby, I would very much like to put her in a crate and mail her to Budapest.

A well-ventilated crate, with water, food, and cushions inside, but still…

Pushing aside thoughts of Ginger, Jace, and innocent children who should have two parents whose auras are in harmony, I report to Hope St. Claire, the animal sanctuary manager, by the steps leading up to the large deck surrounding her home, to get my assignment for the day.

"Are you comfortable with bigger dogs?" she asks, running a hand through her sun-kissed brown bob. "Because we have four or five that could use a good long walk. I can't put them out in the pasture to run until the fence is fixed."

I follow her finger, gazing across the dog pens to the pasture, where one very fine, very bare male back is stretching and flexing as his muscled arms swing a giant hammer, pounding a fence pole into place in a manly display that sends a shiver across my skin. My body immediately perks up, admiring every gorgeous inch of him, even as my brain firmly whispers *no*.

I can't drool over Jace O'Dell like this.

He's not meant to be mine. I have to get over him, once and for all, no matter how irresistibly strong and sexy he is, or how much I miss his smile, or how intense the connection between us is every time our eyes meet.

It doesn't matter how many mantras I chant to keep my root chakra in balance and my sexual energy in check when it comes to this man. Every time I see him my pulse quickens, my mouth goes dry, and I'm overcome with a need to *know* him again. In every way, including the naked and rolling around on the floor of his bar making love in a shaft of moonlight kind of way…

But I can't confide in Cassie. And I can't tell Savannah, my best friend in the entire world, either. Even though we met when she was filming *Savannah Sunshine* in California, she was mostly raised here in Happy Cat, and she knows *everyone* here and I know she'd be tempted to tell tales. Plus, she would sense how unusually distraught I am, get worried, and probably end up rushing home. And after her horrible divorce, she deserves all the time she needs to heal and get happy in England.

I'm just going to have to overcome this on my own, to

forget Jace O'Dell exists, or that I foolishly thought he might be my Kindred Penis, or that he helped bring Princess von Spooksalot and Sir Pendleton into my life.

Which reminds me, I need to move Sir Pendleton to a higher shelf, where he'll be safe, and out of Princess's reach. Her crush on him is kind of cute, but I don't think the stuffy, proper Sir returns her affections.

Which is fine.

Love doesn't always flow both ways in life. It's a cruel fact, but a fact nevertheless.

"Olivia?" Hope says, blinking concerned, melted-chocolate eyes my way.

I snap my head back to her with a cheerful, *nothing's wrong here* smile. "Yes! Yes, I can walk dogs. I love walking dogs. All at once, or one at a time?"

Hope holds up a finger. "One at a time. They like to play when they're together, and they're seriously *large* dogs."

She glances behind me, her eyes going dreamy around the edges as a familiar voice says, "Tech support here, reporting for duty."

Uh-oh. I know *that* look, that feeling.

It rushes through me every time I look at Jace.

The O'Dell brothers apparently have that effect on a lot of women, I realize, as Blake O'Dell, one of Jace's younger brothers, ambles up the stone path leading from the parking lot. He's in overalls with his sun-streaked brown hair hanging below his shoulders, but his normal smile missing in action. He glances at his wristwatch. "What did you break this time, Shock Doc?"

Hope's smile falls away. "I told you, I don't have my vet's license. And the main PC in the office won't boot up."

"Got it. Hey, Olivia," Blake says. "Way to shake things

up around here. You ask me, moon-bathing should be legal. Naked is natural. Right, Hope?"

She sputters, coughs, and almost falls off the bottom step before she grabs hold of the wooden railing and nods. "Totally. But I'm glad she's here. And dressed. For her own safety. It's hard to get good help and the mosquitos are bad today. Wouldn't want a bite in the wrong place."

"And I'm happy to be here," I say.

Blake gives me a shoulder hug, tells me to, "keep my chin up," and bounds up the stairs, headed for the main office in what used to be Hope's laundry room.

And now Hope's scowling at his retreating back, her cheeks pink, reminding me of Cassie when she was still in her "Ryan O'Dell is the most frustrating man on the planet" phase.

I wish I found Jace frustrating. It might be easier to resist him.

But I don't. I find him adorable and delicious and so pounce-able I'm seriously reconsidering whether my spirit animal is a crane, the way I've always thought, or something more feline. Like a bobcat. Or a puma, all sleek and golden and ready to tackle unsuspecting menfolk to the ground at a moment's notice.

My eyes try to slide Jace's way, but I exert superhuman control, forcing them to stay on Hope's flushed face as she says, "Where were we?" She snaps her fingers. "Right. The dogs. Come meet Alex. She's going stir-crazy, so I'll have you walk her first."

Alexis, aka Alex, is a massive baby, with paws the size of my hands and black spots over gray fur. "She's a Great Dane-Lab mix, and she's still a puppy," Hope tells me, laughing as the dog begins to squirm in excitement at having two people waiting outside her kennel. "Who's a good girl? That's right. Alex is a good girl." Hope reaches down to pop the latch on the enclosure.

Alex lunges, wrapping her paws around my neck as she lavishes me with puppy kisses

"Oh, sweet baby! Nice to meet you too." I rub her fur while she continues to lick my face like I'm the most delicious human she's ever encountered, until I'm laughing so hard I sneeze all over both of us—once, twice, three times, until Alex releases me with a whimper.

"Oh, no. Allergies?" Hope asks.

I stand, shaking my head as I sniff and blink. "No, I've never been allergic to anything."

She smiles ruefully. "Welcome to Georgia, hon. It was bound to happen sooner or later. Nature does it's best to kill us around here, but we like it. Keeps us in our place, you know?"

I laugh as she gets Alex clipped to her leash. I promise to check in when I get back to see who's next in the walking queue, and the puppy and I head off in the opposite direction of where Jace is working.

But I can still feel him there.

And a teensy tiny peek over my shoulder confirms that he's still not wearing his shirt.

Meditation. That's what I need. More meditation in my daily routine. If I stay focused on the present moment, then I won't think about Jace's kiss or his hands or how amazing it felt to be naked with him, even on the sticky floor of the bar.

I can do this.

I can get over him.

I have to. He has a baby on the way. And the baby needs him. So I will step aside and quit mooning and dreaming and remembering the look on his face when I kissed him.

Like he was *honored*.

No one's ever *honored* by me. Especially not here.

I love Happy Cat. It's warm and friendly and a little weird. And though not everyone loves that Savannah built Sunshine Toys here, and even fewer people vibe with my way of seeing the world, they're still so nice. Ruthie May at the factory, and her family, and Cassie and Ryan and all the shop owners around the square—they're a big happy family. Dysfunctional at times, yes, but what family isn't? And as a person who's all alone in the world, without any living family of my own, I'm so grateful that they've adopted me and made me one of their tribe.

Even if they think I'm ditzy. Or odd. Or, occasionally, flat-out crazy.

Alex and I reach the far edge of the field and turn to follow the edge of the woods surrounding the farm. She's such a happy dog, occasionally lunging to chase a squirrel or a leaf, but I rein her in and we stay on course. Gradually, we relax in each other's company, chatting about the weather and when Mercury will be in retrograde, and if I should do star charts for more of the animals here, like I did for George Cooney the night Jace made love to me, when I was too excited to sleep because I was certain I'd found something special. Some*one* special.

No. *Bad* thoughts. It's okay to have the memory, but it's not okay to let the memory own me. I need to stay in the present moment, acknowledge it, and let it pass.

I repeat the mantra to myself a few times. "Acknowledge it and let it go. Acknowledge it and let it go…"

Alex barks in agreement.

"That's right, Alex. Acknowledge it and—*aaahh!*"

I don't see the llama barreling our way until it's almost on top of me. It's skipping gracefully, but crazy fast, and mooing—*mooing?*—at me, its eyes alight with affection. I scramble away, obeying the self-preservation instinct that insists I run first and ponder the danger level of llamas later.

I don't know anything about llamas, but this one is big and fluffy and its tongue is hanging out. And the faster I run, the faster it pursues.

I glance over my shoulder to see it gaining on me. I don't know why it's loose or where it came from, but Alex is barking her head off, yanking me back and forth across the uneven ground. The next time I look back, my foot catches on a rock, and I squeal as I topple over, crashing into something cold and wet.

I'm struggling to right myself with a dog licking my neck and a llama licking my face—so maybe not so dangerous, after all—when I hear my name. "Olivia! Get. Back. Shoo! Shit, Olivia, are you okay?"

That voice.

Those eyes.

That strong grip pulling me out of the water trough.

Am I okay?

Nope.

I am definitely not okay.

FOUR

Jace

My pulse is racing, fear that Olivia's been hurt making it feel like my heart is about to punch a hole in my chest. And then she looks up at me, and it stops.

My heart just...stops.

And it isn't just because she's the most beautiful woman ever to fall into a water trough and get slobbered on by an alpaca and a dog at the same time. It's because she looks straight through to my soul, as if the walls I've built to keep the world at a distance don't exist.

Our eyes meet and she sees me and I see her too.

I see that she still wants me as much as I want her. Even though we've been avoiding each other, doing our best to pretend that night at the bar never happened. But it did and I can't breathe the same air as this woman without thinking of how much I want to touch her, kiss her, feel her body melting into mine as she takes me to that sexy, laughter-filled place I've only found with her.

And not just because we were both accidentally drunk.

At least, I hope not…

"Dr. Peppy," I blurt out as I grab the dog's leash, shushing her gently while I hold the alpaca at bay with my other arm. But the alpaca—Chewpaca, I think Hope said its name was—is having none of it. He darts around me, getting another lick in on Olivia's bare shoulder as she struggles out of the trough.

She blinks, swiping water droplets from her forehead. "No, that's Alexis, Alex for short. I'm not sure what the llama's name is."

"Alpaca," I say, proving I have the conversational skills of a caveman. I clear my throat, getting a tighter hold on Alex's leash as she lunges for Olivia, before I add, "Chewpaca is an alpaca. Just moved in yesterday from Hope's grandma's farm and has already broken the fence in three places. But I'm pretty sure he's harmless."

"Of course he is. Chewpaca seems very sweet. Slobbery, but sweet." She laughs nervously, avoiding my eyes as she squeezes water from her hair, and I do my best not to let my gaze veer south of her pretty face. Her shirt was once pale yellow, but it's now practically see-through. At least enough for me to know that she isn't wearing a bra.

Dear Lord, give me strength.

I will not look at Olivia's chest.

I won't even *think* about Olivia's chest, even though it's the most beautiful chest I've ever seen, and I want to trace her freckle constellation with my tongue so badly my jaw is starting to ache.

But I'm going to be a father, and despite the fact that Ginger and I aren't getting along any better than we were two weeks ago, when she dropped the baby bomb in my lap, we're committed to making things work as a family. We're still not sure what that family is going to look like — whether we'll be living together or trying something else — but I'm committed to at least trying the traditional route. I know not every kid has a mother and father in the same house, but I want to give our baby the best shot possible. He or she is already going to be the offspring of the town fuck-up—I can't even take a leak without getting arrested —the very least I can do is give my son or daughter a stable, traditional start in life.

Before they grow up and get wise enough to wish they'd been born to Ryan or one of the more desirable O'Dell brothers.

"So who's Dr. Peppy?" Olivia asks, stroking Chewpaca's back while he makes some very horny-sounding mooing noises that do nothing to help me keep my focus where it belongs.

"What?" I blink and tell Alex to "sit," a command she ignores, continuing to strain at her leash, trying to wiggle between Olivia and Chewpaca and get in on the petting action. "No, it isn't a someone. It's the bar... That night we stayed late..." I shake my head. "I've been meaning to tell you. There was a mix up with the soda delivery. The supplier accidentally gave us Dr. Peppy instead of Dr Pepper. Dr. Peppy's a new cider out of Atlanta. Tastes just like Dr Pepper only with eight percent alcohol by volume."

Her brows lift. "Oh, wow. That's crazy."

I nod, studying her face as I add in a softer voice, "So maybe we were drunker than we thought. I had a glass too, while I was loading the dishwasher. And that shot of tequila."

"Oh, I..." She presses her lips together, leaning her forehead against Chewpaca's neck as she adds in a voice almost too soft to hear, "I don't think I was drunk, but I'm sorry if I took advantage. I certainly never meant to."

Before I can assure her that the last thing I felt that night was taken advantage of, a siren whoops from across the pasture, followed by a voice over a loudspeaker saying, "Doesn't look like the public is being served, O'Dell. Less talking to pretty girls and petting the ponies, more chopping wood and building fences."

My teeth grind together, but instead of flipping the bird to Deputy Chester Roten—pronounced Roh-tin, but he'll always be Rotten in our hearts—I turn and wave. He's my arresting officer, after all, and the more I piss him off, the more he's going to look for a chance to nail my ass to the wall again.

"Is that man blind?" Olivia murmurs with a cluck of her tongue. "Clearly Chewpaca is a llama or alpaca, not a pony."

"Nope. Not blind, just dumb," I say through gritted teeth, keeping my smile in place as I hand Alex's leash back to her. "And spiteful. So I'd better get back to pounding fence before he starts more trouble. I'll put Chewpaca back in the paddock on my way, let you and Alexis get back to your walk without anyone getting licked to death."

She sighs. "Okay. Thank you."

"You're welcome." I loop an arm around the alpaca's neck. "Come on, Chewpaca, let's get you back where you belong." The alpaca groans pitifully, straining back toward Olivia, but I keep a gentle, but firm, grip on him as I turn back to the front of the property. "See you later, Liv. Take care of yourself."

"You too," she says as I walk away, willing myself not to turn and look back, not to see her standing there looking like an angel and something from my dirtiest dreams all wrapped into one. "And, Jace!"

Heart leaping, I turn.

"I'm sorry," she says. "For taking advantage."

"You didn't," I promise, my voice thick with all the things I want to say to her, but can't. Things like "that was the best night of my life," and "I'd give anything to live it over again, even if it ended in getting arrested a second time."

Instead, when she asks, "You swear?" I say, "I swear," and force myself to turn and walk away.

I'm trying. I really fucking am, but I'm never going to get her out of my head at this rate. Being forced to see her every weekend at community service, running into her in town, catching glimpses of her riding her scooter past the bar, looking ridiculously adorable with a flowered scarf in her hair and a hedgehog—also in a flowered scarf—riding in her sidecar.

Apparently, Princess enjoys the wind in her quills almost as much as she enjoys humping taxidermied squirrels. Cassie let the last part slip during family dinner at my folks' place the other night, making Mom and Pops laugh so hard Mom almost peed her pants. Cassie can tell a story, but I couldn't help wishing I'd heard it all from Olivia. That I'd been able to laugh with her over the story, or even see it go down in person. Not because I'm some sort of pervert who enjoys watching weird interspecies mating rituals with disturbing necrophilia overtones, I just wish I were spending time with Olivia.

At her house, with her pets, in close proximity to her bed...

"Stop it, asshole," I grumble, earning a grunt from Chewpaca. "No, not you," I say, patting him on the neck as I let him back into the paddock he somehow managed to escape à la an alpaca Houdini. "Me. I'm the asshole."

As if to prove my point, a high-pitched voice croons

from the parking lot, "Jacey, I'm here. Brought your lunch. Fried bologna and cheese with extra mustard, just like you like it."

"Thanks! Be right there," I say, forcing a smile.

I have never enjoyed fried bologna—I'd rather eat a dried cat turd on a rice cake, in fact—but somewhere along the way Ginger got it in her head that I love the stuff. And once Ginger gets something in her head, there's no talking her out of it. She's as stubborn as she is committed to making us work.

At least today, and for the past two weeks, once she realized she was pregnant and that it was time to stop playing games and lock it down with me. Before the test came back positive, she enjoyed keeping me guessing.

Flirting with other guys just enough to drive me crazy—enough that I broke it off for the hundredth time or she broke it off, citing my "jealous anger" as a deal-breaker—used to be her favorite hobby.

Now, she's super into bringing me lunch. And showing up at my house wearing nothing but a raincoat with lingerie underneath.

She says the pregnancy hormones are making her horny, which is just my luck lately. Most guys get a partner who's busy puking her guts out; I get a not-quite-ex-not-quite-girlfriend who's rabid for my cock, right when my cock has decided he's not interested in sex anymore.

At least not with Ginger. We haven't slept together since our trip to Mexico two and a half months ago before we broke up—again. Since before that night with Olivia, the night I thought was going to change everything.

If I'm serious about giving my kid the traditional, mommy-and-daddy-live-together happy home life, I'll have to start sleeping with Ginger again, sooner or later. And she'll probably want to get married, even though she's the one who put me off the last time I hinted at taking the next step, a good two years ago, when things were still more good than bad between us.

But back then she made it clear she wasn't ready to settle down with a guy with my reputation. She never said anything outright, but from that day on I had the ugly suspicion that she was keeping her options open, waiting for someone better than me to come along.

My run-in with Chester the Rotten Copper wasn't the first. He's pinged me for everything from having a taillight out to playing my music too loud to fighting in the bar when I was trying to play bouncer, not participant. But with my reputation, it didn't matter what I was trying to do—all because I gave the guy a flushie in high school when he wouldn't quit pestering Emma June about taking her to Homecoming. Ryan said I should've had a man-to-man with him instead. Clint said I should've made sure he didn't see my face while I was flushing his head down the toilet. Blake didn't notice I was feuding with anyone in high school because he had his nose in a book.

And now I'm the town's bad boy with a reputation and a record.

Ginger could do better. Wouldn't have taken much for her to find a guy with a nicer track record, and she's always looking.

Or she was.

Until the baby.

I meet her in the parking lot, because I know she's not going to get her strappy heels dirty by walking over to meet me. She's showing off miles of legs under her short skirt, but instead of imagining a trip to happy valley between those legs, all I see is a long-ass drive ahead of me.

"Here's your lunch, baby," she says, fluffing her chest higher in her tight white tank and leaning into me.

I back up. "I'm filthy, Ginger."

"I know, I don't care," she purrs. "Are you coming over for dinner? I'm making your favorite..." She gives me a saucy wink and rolls one shoulder. "Dessert."

I wait for my dick to respond, but he curls up in the fetal position.

It's for the baby, I remind him.

He gives me the middle finger.

I've touched Ginger plenty of times—obviously—but when our fingers brush as she hands me the brown paper bag with a fried heart attack lovingly prepared inside it, I have to fight the urge to recoil.

We're not right.

We've never *been* right—we've always spent as much time fighting as having fun and it's a pattern that's only gotten worse with time.

But it's too late to turn back now. That ship sailed the day those two pink lines popped up in her pregnancy test. Still, I find I can't fake any lovey-dovey shit right now. Not with Olivia's sweet face still so fresh in my memory.

I gesture to the fence. "Gotta get back to it before Deputy Roten decides to extend my sentence," I say gruffly. "Thanks. For lunch."

"Dinner's at five," she replies.

"Gotta open the bar tonight," I remind her. "It's Saturday."

She pouts. "Can't you have someone else handle it? What about your bar girl—what's her name? With the nose?"

"That rules out a lot of people," I deadpan, though I know she's talking about my bar back with a schnozz as big as her heart. "Poppy's a good kid, but she's not ready to handle a Saturday night crowd."

"Oh, come on, she can get people beers. It's not that

hard. And I really want to spend some quality time with you." She strokes a finger down my chest, and my cock whimpers in protest.

Stop it, I tell it. *You're being an asshole.*

My dick snorts and casts a meaningful look over his shoulder, clearly insinuating that I've got him confused with someone else, while my asshole lodges a formal complaint with H.R., citing abusive language in the work environment and general disparagement of his character amongst his grievances. And somewhere in the dark recesses of my mind, a voice that sounds like my fifth-grade teacher, Mr. Lumpus, insists that I've lost my mind.

Possible, Mr. Lumpus. Very possible.

Aloud, I hear myself say, "All right. I'll see if I can get someone to cover, at least the first part of the shift."

Ginger beams brightly. "Good. Because I have something *extra* special planned for you."

She turns to sashay back to her car, hooking a thumb in the waist of her skirt and lowering it just enough for me to see that she's not wearing underwear.

No strap where the thong should be.

I should be salivating—Ginger's always had an amazing body.

But I'm just…bored.

And tired.

And facing the rest of my life with a cringing dick and an irritable asshole.

But at the same time I'm so fucking excited about the baby. *My* baby. My flesh and blood, who'll come into this world with no strikes against him. Or her. I want to give that kid every single opportunity I can afford to give her, and probably a few I can't.

I just wish…

I shake my head and turn back toward the fence, brown

paper bag in hand, and remind myself that wishing isn't going to solve anything.

This is my life. This is reality.

I need to quit looking at Olivia, who's chatting with Chester the Asswipe and shaking her head at Hope as she reaches for another dog's leash, clearly intending to complete her day of service, even if she's soaking wet and covered in alpaca spit, because she's just *that* much of a class act.

I need to stop wishing I were meeting her for dinner tonight. Or taking her out for those vegetarian tacos she likes, and then back for Netflix and chill at my place.

She sneezes three times in rapid succession, making me flinch, and I realize that I'm starting to get a boner from standing here thinking about feeding her tacos.

I jerk my head away and tighten my grip on Ginger's lunch.

I've made my bed.

I have to sleep in it.

And it looks like *sleeping* is all I'll be doing.

FIVE

From the text messages of Jace and Clint O'Dell

Clint: Bro. WTF? I'm in Japan, not dead. Why didn't you tell me about what's going down with you and Ginger?

Jace: Denial?

Clint: Dude.

Jace: I know.

Clint: *profanity emoji*

Jace: Don't send those cartoon things. WTF is wrong with you?

Clint: WTF is wrong with me? You. GINGER. *carrot emoji* BABY. *baby emoji* And Ryan says you're going to *bride emoji* any day now. What the fresh steaming hell, man?

Jace: I know. I KNOW, okay? Stop with the emoji vomit.

Clint: Then talk. Explain this shitstorm to me so it makes sense.

Jace: A kid deserves two parents. So I'm going to make this work. I'm gonna be a dad and dads make sacrifices.

Clint: But Ginger. GINGER!

Jace: Not helping.

Clint: Not sure I'm trying to.

Jace: Somebody damn well needs to. I get it, none of you have ever been Ginger fans, and no, this isn't ideal. But I'm gonna be a father. To a kid who's probably gonna need way more than I can give, but I've gotta at least give it my best shot.

Clint: Jace. You're gonna be an awesome dad.

Jace: Yeah? Why so sure? I fuck pretty much everything else up. Ask any "book club" group in town and they'll tell you I've danced with the devil one too many times to be fit for polite company.

Clint: Fuck those gossips. You're not a dumb teenager lashing out at authority anymore. You're a respectable business owner in a small town that gossips too much. But you pay your taxes, you bathe regularly, and you're going to start flossing before you're forty.

Jace: Dude, I floss. Every day.

Clint: See! You've got the dad thing in the bag.

Jace: I thought so yesterday, but today…

Clint: What?

Jace: I'm trying. I want to do what's right, but Ginger invited me over for dinner and "dessert" tonight, and I begged off. I said… Shit, I can't even type it.

Clint: YOU TOLD HER YOU HAVE A HEADACHE?

Jace: I told her an alpaca sneezed on me and that it might have been carrying some kind of bacteria that would be bad for the baby.

Clint: *crying laughing emoji*

Jace: Looking for support here, asshole.

Clint: Sorry. Sorry. But—bro. AN ALPACA SNEEZE?

Jace: It just came out, and I couldn't take it back. I told her I'd get in touch with Hope and see how long I might be contagious. And then I hung up like a fucking coward. And now I'm at work wearing a mask over my face in case Ginger comes in to check on me and everyone keeps asking if I've got the summer flu and I have to nod and act interested in all their homemade remedies. Like drinking live tadpoles mixed with lemon juice and honey.

Clint: That's messed up.

Jace: I know. It would be bad enough if the tadpoles were dead.

Clint: No, I mean the shit with Ginger. You flat-out lied to your baby mama.

Jace: Well, what the hell was I supposed to do? I have to marry her, I get that and I'm willing, but I don't want to sleep with her anymore. I literally CAN'T. She tries to kiss me and my dick just shrivels up like a thirty-year-old pickle.

Clint: *pickle emoji*

Jace: STOP.

Clint: You deserved that one. I didn't need that mental image of your pants pickle.

Jace: WTF am I going to do?

Clint: Get a strap-on from the factory and only bang in the dark?

Jace: I hate you. And I have to go.

Clint: Wait, wait. You were at the animal sanctuary today, right? Because you're a pee-pee perpetrator?

Jace: No, because Chester is a dick. Nobody was around. I needed to take a leak. And he fucking wrote me up for GEORGE pissing in public too, and the trash panda's not even my pet. Seriously, it's not like we were murdering babies. And then the judge, who is also an asshat, threw out George's citation, but decided I deserved community service while the trash panda deserved a snack. Even though I'm betting that little shit is at least as smart as I am. I swear, he started laughing when the verdict came down.

Clint: Yeah. Heard all that. Agree that George probably has you beat IQ-wise, but you were at the farm sanctuary. Today. That's the point. Did you see Blake?

Jace: Briefly. He was doing candy-ass work in the air conditioning.

Clint: Heh. Interesting.

Jace: What?

Clint: What do you mean, "What?" Are you blind?

Jace: Sometimes I wish. Like when I walked in on Mom and Dad last week. I was early for dinner and Dad had Mom up on the kitchen counter.

Clint: FUCKER. Now I'm picturing *that* and your pants pickle. Thanks. *barfing emoji*

Jace: They were getting the jars down from the top shelf. For pickling okra. What did you think I meant?

Clint: *knife emoji* *profanity emoji* *heart emoji* *clown emoji* *poop emoji*

Jace: FINE. You win. What the fuck is so "interesting" about Blake being at the sanctuary? He does IT temp work for a lot of businesses around town.

Clint: Nah, you don't want to know. Bad enough you have to watch Ryan and Cassie being in love while your pants pickle is broken.

Jace: This is what I get for not telling you about them myself, isn't it?

Clint: You've got your own problems. I'll ask Ryan to spy on Blake for me and tell me why the fuck he keeps bitching about Hope like it's his third part-time job. He'll love that shit. And Ryan enjoys taking an interest in other people's lives.

Jace: When's the last time you got laid, Betty McGossip?

Clint: We're talking about your sex life, not mine.

Jace: You know what really sucks? If I could take back the last two months with Ginger, turn back time to before the baby was conceived...I wouldn't. I'm honestly excited to be a dad. I just wish...

Clint: That it wasn't her?

Jace: Gotta go. Need my rest so I can shake this bacteria the alpaca put on me.

Clint: We all wish it wasn't her, but we're not gonna make this harder on you than it already is. We've got your back, Jace. Hang in there. It'll work out.

Jace: You believe that, or are you saying it for my sake?

Clint: Does it matter?

Jace: Nah. Thanks, bro.

Clint: Anytime. Now go pull your head out of your ass, and good luck with your pickle dick. *pickle emoji* *eggplant emoji* *fist bump emoji*

SIX

Olivia

When Savannah asked me to move to Happy Cat with her to help open a sex toy factory after my mom died, I didn't even have to consult my star chart to know it was a good idea. What's *not* to love about a business that promotes love and pleasure, in all their beautiful forms? Plus, Savannah's been my best friend since we were little, when my mom did the makeup for Van's TV show. Now she's the closest thing I have to family. So moving to the town where she was born, where she spent her time when she wasn't filming *Savannah Sunshine* when we were kids, was the most natural decision in the world.

But the factory's been through some rough times lately, especially with Savannah needing personal time to recover from her awful divorce, and all the intrigue of the past few weeks. We need an image revamp almost as much as we need the Self-Warming Lube back in stock, so I have a new job at Sunshine Toys.

I give "Get to Know Us, You'll Love Us!" tours of the factory, converting skeptics into fans and delighting our already established followers with tales from behind the scenes.

By four o'clock, I'm finishing my fourth tour of the day, showing a group of elderly ladies from Atlanta the dildo design studio and lube flavor-testing lab. They're all in pastel business suits and flowered hats—they told their husbands they were going to a flower show in Macon—and are having a great time on their naughty field trip. I can tell.

"Do you use live models for the dildo designs?" the lady in the lavender suit asks.

"Or just some of the cute local boys?" Pink Suit adds, making the rest of the group twitter with laughter.

Cute local boys…

Great. And now I'm thinking of Jace naked in the design studio while I lean over his hard cock, measuring his length and girth while he whispers all the wonderfully intimate things he'd like to do to me. Which makes me wonder if he'd like to play "serious scientist and naughty test subject" with me—I would be the serious scientist, of course, because wearing glasses makes me frisky—and what his favorite flavor of lube is.

Stop thinking about lube. Or at least start talking about it while you're thinking about it. The tourists are waiting!

I shake myself and explain the scientific research that goes into dildo shaping to my rapt audience, determined not to think anymore about Jace.

Because thinking about Jace is *bad*.

He's committed to someone else and having a baby with her, and I'm in danger of serious energetic misalignment if I don't stop thinking about him.

I finish the tour without any further unhealthy fantasizing, then fetch Princess from my small office and carry her down to the Vespa. "Did you have a good time playing in the drawer today?" I ask her.

She snuffles back at me, telling me all about her adventures in napping on her pillow, eating her lunch, snacking on a spider she drowned in her water bowl—a little dark, but she's omnivorous and a wild creature so who am I to judge her for taking her snacks where she can get them?—and then I think she says something about humping the ball I gave her in erotic exploration. Which would be good. Better a ball than Sir Pendleton. She was out of her cage again this very morning, endangering her life by crawling up to the top of the bookshelf to make not-so-sweet love to the stuffed squirrel's leg.

Sir Pendleton was kind about it, but his moustache was cocked at a judgmental angle when we left.

Hopefully a day alone in the house has soothed his frazzled nerves.

I put Princess in her basket in the Vespa's sidecar, tie her tiny scarf in place over her head to keep her quills from getting too ruffled, and we take off for Sunshine Square in the middle of town. It's farmer's market day, and I'm nearly out of fresh honey. I'm also hoping I'll run into Hope while I'm there. I want to talk to her about Princess's diet and slightly out-of-the-ordinary sexual penchants. I mean, love is love and all, but if she's going to have a crush on a squirrel, I'd feel a lot more comfortable if he were alive.

A block after we leave the factory, I spot a familiar profusion of red curls stepping out of a doctor's office, and dread slices through my heart.

It's Ginger.

Leaving what looks like an OB's office, judging from a quick glance at the sign.

Probably having a checkup on her baby.

Jace's baby.

Sob…

"Accept it and let it go," I whisper to myself. "You are a river, constantly in motion, leaving the past behind."

Ginger looks straight at me, her eyes narrowing. The hatred that spikes sharply from her aura in response is so intense it makes me veer to the left, swinging out into oncoming traffic. I recover quickly, concentrating on driving, while the driver in the oncoming car honks and shouts something I don't catch from his open window, but my heart is in my throat and my maternal instincts are screaming that Princess could've been injured.

I should be more terrified at how close I came to death by Cadillac, but Ginger's rage vibes are almost scarier. If I didn't know better, I'd think she'd like to skin me alive. Or worse.

But surely, I must be reading her wrong, projecting my own angst into her energy field or something. Because while she and Jace aren't compatible, everyone in Happy Cat loves Ginger. She's a *kindergarten* teacher, and kindergarten teachers are inherently incapable of evil. And she's a good one too, apparently. Makes her own homemade play dough with sparkles in it and everything.

"I'd like some sparkly play dough," I whisper to Princess. "Or a week-long, all-expenses-paid trip to a meditation retreat. I need some Zen in a major way."

Her headscarf waving in the wind, Princess huffs in empathetic agreement. As if she, too, could use a week-long meditation retreat.

When we arrive at the square, I tuck my hedgehog into a tiny baby sling I made especially for her—complete with slivers of black tourmaline sewn into the lining to help keep her calm during potentially spook-inducing public encounters—and pull on my largest pair of sunglasses.

I haven't been to the farmer's market since the incident with the sno-cones, and I'm trying to go incognito.

I'm also hoping the glasses will mute external focus, helping me to open my third eye, freeing my sixth chakra, the gateway to intuition. Or at least keep me from thinking about sex all the time.

Bad, root chakra. So, so bad...

I've barely stepped foot in the square before George Cooney waddles past with a rainbow ruffle around his neck and a bowling pin painted yellow tucked under his arm. He casts a glance up at me, eyeballing my sling. He looks like he wants to say hi to Princess, but before I can kneel down to bring them face-to-face, I sneeze—hard, in rapid succession—sending George skittering to hide behind the nearest trash can.

Princess squeaks in concern.

"I'm fine," I assure her with a sniff as George chucks the bowling pin into the trash. "Good boy, George. Keep picking up litter," I add. Because that's normal. A bowling pin isn't typical litter, but this is Happy Cat, and a bowling pin is better than the dildos that were strewn all over the square a few weeks ago.

Back on the fateful day that I saw Jace for the first time since I learned that Ginger was having his baby...

When I had to put on a brave, non-devastated face, and pretend nothing was wrong while we all pitched in to fix our little town. Even though my heart was aching with a hurt too deep for any dildo to ever pleasure away.

I sneeze again.

Maybe Hope's right, and I'm coming down with seasonal allergies. I'll have to research homeopathic remedies.

Maud Hutchins from the bakery waves at me as I weave through the booths. I stop to say hi and to ask if she and Gerald need any more samples from the factory, but I don't stand too close, on the chance that I'm sick instead of seasonally affected.

"I'm still working on getting him to try the *first* sample," she whispers, "but I'm making progress." She glances down, her gaze softening. "Oh, is that the hedgehog you found? How's the poor thing doing?"

"She's still a little traumatized from being abandoned." I smile down at Princess, patting her gently on her head. "But we're working on her trust issues with crystal therapy and a lavender diffuser I put near her cage during her mid-morning nap. Hedgehogs are naturally nocturnal, but she's bridging the day and night time worlds like a champ."

"Well, she's a lucky girl to have you to help her. Bread? Gerald baked it this morning."

We discuss which loaves would go well with the chickpea salad I'm making for dinner, and I pick a sour-dough boule and start toward the honey display, only to stop short not four feet past Maud's stand.

Jace is here. I can sense his presence, feel his aura in the air even before I turn to spot him at work in the picnic shelter at the center of the square a few dozen yards away.

In a tight gray tee shirt, faded jeans, and work boots, his body is a graceful temple of human perfection — strong and capable, whether he's serving drinks, hammering fence posts, or doing something as mundane as reaching up to change a light bulb. And he's hiding a huge heart under that grumpy bartender exterior. Chester lives to tell me how many times Jace has been arrested, but I know Jace is one of the good guys.

The laws don't always get it right, and people make mistakes, but mistakes don't define who we are.

Why can't the rest of the town see what a wonderful person he is?

"How many bartenders does it take to screw in a light-bulb?" Cassie appears beside me, making me jump so high my feet actually leave the ground.

I recover quickly and paste a smile onto my lips. "I was meditating."

"About Jace?"

"About the sky," I fib. No good will come of Cassie knowing I can't stop thinking about Jace, *and* I *need* to stop thinking about Jace.

"Are you okay?" she asks, concern coloring her brown eyes behind her glasses.

"I'm—" I start to say *great*, but a giant sneeze steals the word.

People scatter around me, seeking cover, except Ruthie May, who rushes over with a pack of tissues. "You poor thing. Summer cold?"

"No, I don't think—" I sneeze again.

"Sometimes the sunshine makes me sneeze," Ruthie May tuts. "Here. Come sit in the picnic shelter. Oh! You were working at the rescue farm the other day, weren't you? Did you catch the same thing Jace had?"

"Jace was—*achoo!*"

"Caught something from the alpaca," Ruthie May confirms. "Ginger told me all about it. She had a special dinner all made up for him, but he couldn't make it because he didn't want to infect the baby." She claps her hand together in delight. "I'm so excited about the baby! With those two as parents, she'll be cute as a button. Though, Jace will have to work on staying out of trouble now, won't he? But I think he'll come around."

Cassie rolls her eyes.

"He's already come around, as far as I can tell," I say,

but Ruthie May nods in that way that makes it clear she isn't really paying attention as she pulls me to the shelter.

"Here. Sit." She practically shoves me down onto a picnic table bench. "Is that better?"

I'm sitting so close to where Jace stands on another table, screwing a lightbulb into the ceiling, that I can feel the warmth of his energy field flirting with mine. He nods to us, our gazes connect, and my breasts perk up like they're worshipping the moon as my entire body starts to tingle. If I were to touch him right now, I'm pretty sure we'd create actual *visible* sparks of attraction.

This is *not* better. Not at all.

"Hey, Jace," Cassie says. "Thank you for fixing that. It's been out since the last dildo-ball tournament. Teens—good at breaking things, not so good with fixing them."

"Course." He nods again, then goes back to tinkering, all while emitting sex vibes so powerful my pulse starts throbbing in dangerous places. Princess squirms in her carrier against my chest in response, clearly sensitive to my heightened state of agitation.

Two more minutes and we'll probably both be humping someone's leg.

I can't stay here. I've got to get out. "I need to buy hon—hon—*achoo!*"

"Honey?" Cassie asks.

I nod.

"Clover, sourwood, or tupelo?"

"Yes. All of the above." I wipe my nose with the tissue Ruthie May hands over.

"You just sit right there, and I'll go grab those for you, hon," Ruthie May says.

Cassie watches the older woman go, a slight smile playing on her lips. "Anything else you need?" she asks.

I shake my head. "I could have gotten my own honey."

"I know, but Ruthie May loves to help." She squeezes my shoulder and seems about to speak again when something behind me catches her attention and her entire face lights up.

"Go on, I'll be fine," I tell her. I don't need to look over my shoulder to know that Ryan's here, or that he's beaming like only the hopelessly in love can beam, just like his lady. "Give your man a big hug and a kiss and tell him hi for me."

"All right, but if you're not feeling better soon, call me," she says.

Instead of answering, I nod, managing to hold back my sneeze until after she darts off to greet Ryan.

When I'm finished, I pull my sunglasses off to wipe the tears from my eyes and glance down to check on Princess only to instantly realize something is wrong.

Very, very wrong.

One of the carrier straps is broken. The sling is empty.

And I have no idea where my hedgehog has gotten off to.

SEVEN

Jace

"Princess!" Olivia bolts to her feet, bringing trembling fingers to cover her mouth as she spins in a quick circle, searching the ground, her sunglasses tossed aside. "Princess? Princess von Spooksalot?"

I've been trying to play it cool, but when she drags a hand through her hair and goes into another sneezing fit, I'm done.

I hop off the table, putting a hand to her shoulder as she frantically turns the baby sling inside out. The moment we touch, something elemental sends a shock of awareness from my fingers to every inch of my body.

Olivia whips her head up, her breath coming faster and her lips parted. I'm positive she felt it too—that crazy spark —but then she wrenches back, her eyes going wary in a way that punches me in the gut and follows it up with a roundhouse to my kidneys.

"Princess is missing," she whispers. "Maybe she just wandered off. But she could have run away, I guess. She's a lovely little hedgehog, but she has trust issues. But you would too if you were abandoned in the park by people who'd made you think they cared about you."

Fuck.

That's what I did to her, isn't it?

I led her on, made love to her, promised her I felt all the things she felt, and then I abandoned her. Without so much as a decent explanation.

"It'll be okay. Let's go find her." I'm taking a risk—if Ginger sees me with another woman, there will be hell to pay—but finding a hedgehog shouldn't take long. I can do this. For a friend.

I scan the square. If there's a hedgehog on the loose, sooner or later someone's going to start screaming, and we'll just follow the noise. But no one's screaming. Or pointing. Or exclaiming over a newfound pet or possible vermin infestation.

"She's so tiny," Olivia whispers, her voice thick. "Someone could crush her and not even know they'd just committed murder."

"She's going to be fine. She's a fighter." I have no idea if that's true, but it damn well better be. "She found you once. She'll find you again." There. That's more like the *cosmic place in this universe* stuff Olivia believes in. That I'd like to believe in too, if the universe hadn't lifted its leg and pissed all over me one too many times. "Let's backtrack."

I hold out a hand.

She eyes my fingers, but she doesn't reach out, which is probably a good thing for both of us. But she doesn't tell me to go away either.

Instead, she steps out of the shelter and points to the right. "I came up the path from Maud's stand. We got bread, then chatted with Cassie, and I thought I felt her squirming a few seconds ago, but — " She stops and shakes her head. "We should go that way. My gut says that way."

"Hey, Jace," Ryan says behind me. "If you're in Mr. Fix-it mode, the faucet in the firehouse kitchen is still leaking."

I stop and glance back at my big brother. "Get to it next time. Missing hedgehog. Later."

"Oh, no, Princess is missing?" Cassie says with a soft cry of dismay. "Where? We'll help look for her."

We all traipse back to see if Maud's seen a hedgehog, scanning the ground as we go. Nobody is shrieking yet though, so if Princess has been found, it's a quiet sort of found.

"I'll post a note on InstaChat," Cassie says, thumbs tapping at her phone. "Everyone's already been trying to figure out where she came from. They'll want to help look for her."

Maud hasn't seen the hedgehog either, so we split up, Ryan and Cassie heading to the opposite side of the square, while Olivia and I retrace her steps again. She's on the verge of tears, and I'm feeling like fifty shades of slime.

I don't know how I was supposed to stop her hedgehog from sneaking off, the way I used to when I was a teenager, slipping out my window every chance I got, but I still feel like I've let her down.

"George!" she suddenly exclaims. She points to where Ryan's trash panda is waddling his fat ass down the street toward Dough on the Square, Maud and Gerald's bakery. "We should ask George if he's seen Princess."

My lips part, but I can't bring myself to remind Olivia that George, though ridiculously smart, hasn't yet mastered the art of conversation. I owe it to her to stay positive. "Great idea."

If she notices I'm not fully committed to the "Ask George" plan, she doesn't say anything. Instead, she bolts after the pudgy raccoon, who's wearing a clown ruffle today, for some reason, and I bolt after her.

I can't help myself.

She's due north. I'm just following the compass.

We circle around the bakery to find George climbing up on the edge of the dumpster. "George. C'mon, man," I say. "Out of the trash. We need to talk to you.

We need to talk *to you?* I'm losing it, but George doesn't miss a beat before letting out a sharp *chirp-chirp* in response.

I'm pretty sure that was a *fuck you, dude,* but Olivia hears it differently.

"Exactly, George. Princess is missing. Have you seen her?"

He looks between us, his dark eyes seeming to ask *is this lady for real?* before he swishes his tail, and takes a dive into the dumpster to go swimming in the trash.

I shudder. "I can't believe Ryan sleeps with that."

"George takes regular baths," Olivia informs me. "I made Cassie an aromatherapy spritzer to help relax him, and he's enjoying them much more now." She raps on the metal. "George! Please, George, I know you're busy, but we need your help."

I turn away so she can't see me struggling not to wince at the idea of the raccoon giving us dirt on the hedgehog, only to spot a roly-poly bundle of quills hustling across the rear parking lot.

It's Princess, moving fast and dragging a clothesline full of what looks like ladies' delicates toward a giant pothole filled with green sludge.

"Oh, shit." I take off at a run, already seeing that this won't end well. "Stop, Princess!"

"Princess!" Olivia shrieks, breaking into a jog behind me.

I reach the hedgehog first and scoop the buttnugget into my palm, but not before she plucks a pair of hot pink panties off the line, snatching them up in her tiny jaws and drawing them into her tummy as she curls into a ball, shivering in terror. "Hey, little lady, you're okay. I'm not going to hurt you."

I stroke her quills, and by the time Olivia skids to a halt next to us, Princess has poked one tiny pink paw out of her stress ball.

One very mischievous paw, if you ask me. She reaches toward Olivia, snuffling as she clutches the satin panties to her heart with her other three legs, seeming to insist that she's the rightful guardian of all underthings.

If I didn't know better, I'd think this critter was *playing* us.

"Oh, my sweet baby," Olivia gasps, resting a hand on my shoulder that she immediately snatches away, like I've burned her. Or repulsed her.

Fuck.

I hate this. I don't want things to be awkward. I don't want *us* to be awkward. I want…

I just *want*.

"She's okay," I say, holding Princess out for perusal. "All in one piece. And she found herself a pair of panties she likes while she's at it."

Olivia smiles as she leans closer, stroking the hedgehog, who once again extends a paw, clearly loving her new owner almost as much as she loves pink satin.

"Well, at least you're safe now," Olivia whispers. "And I won't tell Maud you stole her panties if you won't." Princess huffs and Olivia nods. "You're right. I don't think pink is her color, either. But I'm going to leave ten dollars in their tip jar next time we come in to make things right."

She straightens, looking me square in the eye, and I lose my breath.

She's so beautiful. And so good-hearted. She makes me want to believe in the better world she sees when she wakes up every morning. In animals that can talk and stones that heal where you hurt and magic waiting around every corner if you're brave enough to look for it.

"Thank you for finding Princess," she whispers. "You're our hero."

I clear my throat, because I'm nobody's hero, not even a hedgehog's. "I had nothing to do with it. It was all you. You're the one who knew to ask George where she went."

Her forehead wrinkles. "You don't really believe George talks to me, do you?" she asks, searching my face.

"Well...no, I don't," I say, unable to lie to her. "But I like that you believe it." I cradle Princess in one hand, lifting the other to brush Olivia's hair from her forehead, my fingertips skimming lightly along her soft skin. "And I want to believe."

"It's okay. You don't have to. I can believe hard enough for the both of us." And then she pushes up on her toes, cupping my cheeks as she presses a sweet, sinful kiss to my lips that makes my entire being ache with wanting her. And I know I should pull away—I'm not a free man, not anymore—but I don't *want* to pull away.

I'm not in love with Ginger, and I'm pretty sure she knows it. Until a few weeks ago, she hadn't said the words in months either. Maybe, once upon a time, what we had was love, but now it's a shadow, a memory without the substance to grow into anything more. We can be friends who care about each other and work together to raise a good kid, but more and more often my gut says that's the best we can hope for—*if* I can keep from pissing her off.

But when Olivia's kissing me, it's hard to care about Ginger's temper, not when everything in the world feels so fucking right.

So I lean into her lips.

And I kiss her back, while I'm cradling her hedgehog in one hand and trying desperately not to touch her with the other. Because if I touch her, I don't think I'll be able to stop touching her, and if I don't stop touching her, I'm going to make love to her, and making love to Olivia again would be a mistake.

Wouldn't it?

I know it would, but I can't seem to remember why, not when she's making those soft, hungry sounds and my blood is rushing fast and she's whispering, "Perfect, so perfect," against my lips.

And it *is* perfect, so much so that I can't help wrapping an arm around her waist and pulling her close. I drag her against me, forgetting all about our little third wheel until she squeals in protest.

"Oh my goodness." Olivia jumps back, slapping a hand over her lips. "Sorry, Princess."

The hedgehog huffs as I glance over my shoulder, breath rushing out as I check to make sure no one saw us.

In this town, someone *always* sees. And then they talk.

"And sorry to you too. I was just— I didn't— I mean, *thank you*," Olivia sputters. "Thank you, again. For helping me."

She gathers the hedgehog into her hands, and that arc of connection flares between us again as our fingers brush, making us both flinch and sigh.

But we can't do this, no matter how much we might want to. At least not until I have a long talk with Ginger and plot a path forward that doesn't involve promising each other 'til death do us part.

"So…friends?" I ask.

"Friends."

I nod, stomach hardening into an unhappy knot. "Friends." Shit. She said that. *I* said that. We both said that. And it's for the best. For now. It *is*, but I don't like it one fucking bit.

She nods. Then shakes her head. And sneezes twice, looking as miserable as I feel.

"I should take Princess home," she says. "She's had a big day."

"I'm glad we found her."

She smiles. "Me too."

I'm rubbing my neck and pushing up and down on the balls of my feet, and I want to go drink myself into oblivion, because I can't do this.

I can't be Olivia's friend.

"Thank you," she sputters again, and then she's gone, dashing around the building, leaving me to pace back and forth in front of the giant pothole before I head over to the Wild Hog for the after-work rush.

Because my cock, the one that shrivels into a fucking pickle when Ginger looks at me? Well, he needs a few minutes to cool down.

EIGHT

Olivia: I'm lost, Savannah. Lost. Adrift on a sea of bad karma without a paddle or a life jacket or a rose quartz grounding crystal in sight. I need sister-friend advice.

Savannah: What?! You? Bad Karma? I don't believe it. You're the queen of good vibes, lady. What's bothering you? Pull up a pint of ice cream and tell Aunt Van all about it.

Olivia: I've already eaten coconut ice cream. And a vegan cookie. And half a bag of homemade granola with extra honey.

Savannah: That sounds serious. Healthy and ethically sourced, but serious...

Olivia: It is. I did something I shouldn't have done and now I can't take it back. And I can't stop thinking about it, no matter what I do. Even guided meditation isn't working. My brain keeps grabbing my hand and leading me back to the things I shouldn't be thinking about.

Savannah: Have you tried a hot bath?

Olivia: A hot bath would not be a good idea...

Savannah: Why not?

Olivia: Heat is part of the problem, Savannah. It's very... warm here this time of year.

Savannah: Turn up the air conditioning and go for it, mama. I know you worry about using too much energy, but desperate times call for desperate baths. In my book, there's not much a hot bath can't cure. Especially if you bring ice cream into the mix. Hold that thought. I'm going to go start a bath. I've still got two hours before I have to be on kiddo duty. More than enough time for a bath and ice cream for breakfast. I'm so glad you texted!

Olivia: Well, you seem happy. That makes me twenty percent happier than I was five minutes ago. *smiley face emoji*

Savannah: I AM happy. My big sister is madly in love, my evil ex is on his way to jail, the sheep of Happy Cat are safe from his amorous advances, and my company is on the rebound in the court of public opinion. And I'm loving my new job here so much! Beatrice is the sweetest kid in the universe. It's almost enough to make me want to have babies of my own someday. Or just kidnap her and raise her as my own.

Olivia: Lol. You would make the best mom. Though you probably shouldn't joke about kidnapping. Just in case your boss checks your texts.

Savannah: Oh, he would never. Colin is way too busy to have time to bother with the nanny. As long as Beatrice isn't dead, peeing in corners, or setting things on fire, he's happy to leave us to our own devices. And she could probably set things on fire and that would still be okay with him, as long as she didn't set fire to anything in his office.

Olivia: Aw…that's kind of sad.

Savannah: It is. He's a good guy just…distant. But Beatrice has me now and I lavish her with attention. And snuggles. And treats. Which means I will have to be very quiet sneaking into the kitchen for ice cream or she'll hear me… I'm going in now. While I'm creeping, please tell me more about this thing you shouldn't have done, and I will be the judge of whether or not you should feel guilty about it.

Olivia: Oh no, I can't tell you. I really can't. All I can say is that it was bad and I'm pretty sure it's making me unfit to be a pet mother.

Savannah: Ridiculous!

Olivia: I'm serious, Van. Princess von Spooksalot ran away the other day. But it's okay—we found her and brought her home.

Savannah: Thank goodness. I know you're crazy about her. And I'm sure she's crazy about you too. She just needs time to adjust to a loving home after all she's been through.

Olivia: That's what I thought too. But now she won't stop dragging this pair of panties she stole from Maud's clothes-line around the house.

Savannah: Panties? Maud's panties? And how did she come to be in possession of Maud's panties? No, you know what —don't tell me. It's Happy Cat. Of course the hedgehog stole some panties. And why shouldn't she have nice under-things? Every girl wants to dress up and feel fancy once in a while. I'm assuming they're nice panties, right? I mean, I know Maud is getting up there, but I've always seen her as a feisty, cute panties type of gal. Or I would have seen her that way, if I'd taken the time to think about her panties.

Olivia: Yes, they're nice panties. Satin. But Princess doesn't try to wear them. She sleeps with them and eats with them and in between sleeping and eating she drags them up to every window she can reach and chews on them like it's her job. And I'm afraid she's going to swallow some of the satin and her intestines will get impacted and then her health will be at risk, all because I'm a stress case who can't calm down and it's negatively affecting the emotional stability of my adopted hedgehog daughter.

Savannah: Or Princess might just be a bit of...an odd duck. You don't know what she was like before, you know. And she did end up abandoned in a park with a hedgehog shaming sign hung on her cage.

Olivia: Cassie made her another one—I RAN AWAY FROM MY MOM AND SHOPLIFTED PANTIES AND NOW ALL THE PANTIES IN TOWN ARE AFRAID OF ME. She took a picture with Princess wearing it around her neck. I'll forward it to you.

Savannah: Oh please do! That sounds adorable. Beatrice
will love it. Though they call them knickers over here. Not
panties.

Olivia: Cute! I always liked that phrase — don't get your
knickers in a twist.

Savannah: Me too. I also like "I'm chuffed to bits." It means
I'm extremely pleased and delighted.

Olivia: Oh! I love it. That chuffs me to bits. I like being
chuffed to bits!

Savannah: Are you thirty percent happier now?

Olivia: Forty percent!

Savannah: Good! You deserve all the happiness. Have
you talked to Hope St. Claire about Princess? She's so
good with animals. She might have an idea of how to
help.

Olivia: I was going to talk to her the other day, when I was
there for my community service. But she was super busy.
Her computer exploded and then her lawnmower exploded
and then the pinball machine in her garage exploded too. So
she had a lot on her plate.

Savannah: Sounds like it! But she's always had that weird
thing with electronics.

Olivia: It's a super-charged bioenergy field. It's like her
aura took performance enhancing supplements and then
had a few cups of coffee for good measure. My mom's guru

in California used to call people like that Wipers because they're so good at wiping hard drives clean.

Savannah: Of course you know this! I bet Hope's so glad you're there to talk to about stuff like that.

Olivia: We actually haven't had a chance to talk much, but I hope we will. I'm going to stop by tomorrow after work. I hope.

Savannah: Good! You should. And… Shoot, I have to run, babes. Beatrice just stuck her head into the bathroom and is insisting on stealing my tub and my ice cream, the wretched, brilliant little beastie. I just love her! But I can text or call you back in an hour or so if you think you'll still be up.

Olivia: I should head to bed, but thank you. I appreciate the thought and you. You really have cheered me up. I love you and miss you so much.

Savannah: I love and miss you too! We'll talk again soon, okay? We have to plan your trip to come visit this fall. I hear London is magical in autumn!

Olivia: Will do, talk soon!

NINE

Jace

I'd be enjoying my time at the animal sanctuary if Chester wasn't breathing down my neck, it wasn't seven million degrees out here in the Georgia heat, and I wasn't currently wickedly jealous of the alpaca licking Olivia like she's tastier than carrots and apples combined.

Because of course she is. Ten times tastier and twenty times cuter when she laughs, dodging Chewpaca's tongue as he lunges forward, testing the new section of fence I finished this morning.

She's so damn *happy* all the time. A bright, shining beacon of joy, impossible to resist.

But that's what I have to do — resist.

Ginger showed up at the Wild Hog last night, but the words *can we talk* had barely passed my lips before she burst into tears. She sobbed that the pregnancy hormones were making her think I was going to dump her for being ugly as soon as she started showing, and *can we talk* is one of those phrases women hate, and I wasn't abandoning her, was I?

Wasn't like I could follow that with *this relationship isn't working*.

I'm a fuck-up, but I'm not a heartless bastard.

But I can't even look at Olivia without feeling this pull in my heart, like she's where I'm supposed to be. Where I belong. Or maybe it's all wishful thinking. And hell, I've jerked her around so much, who knows if she'd want me even if I were a free man?

She sneezes, and then laughs again when Chewpaca nuzzles her shoulder. He tries to lick her again, and I start to worry that there's something wrong with me that I'm getting turned on watching an animal try to lick the woman of my dreams.

"Hours don't count if you're not working, O'Dell," Chester says behind me.

My shoulders hitch. "Getting a drink," I say, keeping my voice neutral, because I still remember the look on Ryan's face when he bailed me out of jail a few weeks ago.

Just stay out of his way, Ryan had said.

I'm trying, brother. Seriously, I'm trying.

"Well, drink faster," Chester tells me. "I just told Hope to make you shovel out the horse pens."

They're called stalls, I think, but I don't correct him.

I probably owe the bastard a thank you for sparing me another minute standing here, staring at Olivia and longing for things I'll never have.

I start toward the goat pens, which is where I saw Hope last—she's the one signing off on my community service, not Chester. But it takes effort not to watch Olivia. Not even George, waddling by in a rainbow clown wig, while four peacocks follow him down to the pond, is enough of a distraction to make me forget she's here.

I heard her talking to Hope about Princess when I arrived, but Ginger was here too—she says pregnancy makes her love animals, though I can't kick the feeling she's making sure I don't fuck up—so I couldn't hang out and listen in. But I hope the hedgie's okay. I've got a soft spot for her. She reminds me of that night with Olivia, when I was so sure everything was about to change for the better.

I wipe my brow as I step into the shaded goat barn and am about to call out a *hello?* when I hear a familiar voice. "I think I've fixed this milking machine enough times to know what's wrong."

"*Copernicus kicked it.* It didn't blow a fuse!"

Sounds like Blake and Hope are at it again, a fact that makes me determined to kill time until one of them leaves in a huff, as usual. I've got enough angst in my life without getting in the middle of theirs, thank you very much.

Chester isn't following me, so I angle closer into the barn. I can't see the boss lady or my brother—they're around the corner—but I can enjoy the smell of the fresh hay and the shade and relatively cooler temperature while I wait. One of the baby goats bleats at me, and I pause to scratch his head—her head?—while Blake and Hope argue.

"You can't milk a male goat," he growls, "so what was he even doing back here?"

"Do you know what I'd like to see? I'd like to see you try to do everything I do on this farm for *one day.* And then go ahead and ask me how a male goat got back by the milking machines and why my alpaca got out of his fence and who dumped a load of feed in the middle of the parking lot. Go ahead. You try being me for a day and see how well *you* do."

I arch my brows at the baby goat, indicating that I think Hope's got a valid point. The goat bleats again in agreement, obviously well aware that an operation this size can't help but succumb to chaos now and then.

"Sheesh. It was a legitimate question," Blake mutters.

"It's *annoying*. And you sound just like Kyle."

"I. Do. Not. Sound. Like. Kyle."

For the first time in four days, I feel like smiling, because that was funny. Her cousin Kyle is a shithead of high pedigree—he'd never get community service for taking a leak in public because his genes wouldn't allow the thought to cross his mind, and even if it did, he'd use his family money to hire the best lawyers in the country to get him out of it.

He's always been a smug asshole, but it's gotten even worse since his and Hope's grandfather went into a nursing home, and Kyle got unrestricted access to the purse strings.

"Well, you sound like Kyle to me, and my perspective is as valid as yours," she replies, and that's my cue.

Blake's so laid back, sometimes we wonder if he has blood pressure at all, but Hope St. Claire has always been able to get under his skin, and it rarely ends well. I give the goat a final pat and head toward the back part of the barn.

"Oh, yeah?" he asks. "Would Kyle get up at the butt crack of dawn on a Saturday morning to come fix everything that's broken around this place?"

"He would if I called and asked him to."

"Yeah? You think he'd replace your refrigerator in three hours flat, all while keeping your sperm collection on ice, no matter how many times he had to refill the coolers in the damned heat?"

"Yes, he would, because Chewpaca has very valuable sperm."

He snorts. "Fine, but he sure as hell wouldn't drive all the way down to Macon to pick you up after that ancient truck of yours dies *again* because you refuse to get a new one."

"He would. I'm his family."

I almost laugh. Kyle doesn't care about family—and he wouldn't do any of those things—and Hope knows it. She's just baiting Blake.

Not that he doesn't deserve it—he's snippier with her than he is with anyone else, a fact of life I've never understood. I've always liked Hope, and found her super easy to get along with.

"Yeah? You think so?" Blake asks, his voice dangerously quiet, making it clear I need to intervene before blood is shed. "Would Kyle do *this*?"

I turn the corner, ready to referee, only to see my little brother wrap his arms around Hope's waist, pull her in close, and crush his mouth to hers. Instantly, it becomes obvious that I was only getting half the story.

There are visible fireworks going on back here and she is clearly not offended by the kiss.

I mean, not if gripping his shirt and making hungry noises while she devours his mouth like it holds the secrets to the universe can be considered *not offended*.

Pretty sure they're as hot for each other as they are bothered.

And I'm pretty sure I'm gonna forget I just saw this.

I turn on my heel and sneak back toward the entrance, but I'm not quick enough. I'm still in earshot as Hope gasps, "What the hell was that about?"

"Would he?" Blake demands. "Would Kyle do *that*?"

"He's my cousin," she says, her voice a mixture of angry and dreamy. "First cousin. So no, that would be gross."

"You're gross," he says, clearly teasing, at least to my ears, but she doesn't seem to take it that way.

"Thanks," she snaps. "And you're an asshole!"

"Jesus, Hope, I wasn't—"

"Just stop. Stop—*ugh*. I can't even with you. Just fix the damn machine so I can pay you and you can leave and we can pretend that never happened."

I dive out of the barn and out of sight, leaning against the wall beside the door. Olivia's left Chewpaca and is walking Alex again, and even though I'm too far away to hear, I can tell she's talking to the dog.

Probably carrying on a whole conversation, understanding every bark and growl the dog offers in response. Or, if not, making you believe that she can.

Hope strolls out. I count to four, then follow. "Hey, Hope. There you are."

She spins.

Looks at me.

Looks at the barn.

Looks at me.

"I need a new assignment," I tell her.

She looks at the barn again, and once more at me.

I keep my face neutral. Didn't see anything. Don't know anything. Not getting involved.

Got enough problems of my own without turning Gertie Gossip over my brother losing his cool and hate-kissing Hope St. Claire.

She sighs and rubs a hand over her face. "How do you feel about mucking horse stalls?"

"Different shit, same day."

Her flustered smile makes me feel like I'm not a total fuck-up, but it doesn't relieve the pressure that one of Olivia's smiles would relieve. "Great. Thank you. And sorry. And thank you."

"What I'm here for," I tell her.

"And that makes you my favorite O'Dell brother today," she mutters. She blows out a breath that makes a few strands of her hair dance, then gestures to the office. "Let me know when you're done, and I'll sign off on your hours."

I nod and turn to go. Catching sight of Olivia at the far edge of the field again, I sigh. I wonder what she'd say about Blake and Hope's auras. Or their chakras or their stars or their whatevers.

And then I wonder what she'd say about ours.

But as I head around the goat barn to the larger horse shelter, I realize I don't need to ask. I can already feel it in my gut.

Olivia and me?

We're star-crossed.

Not destined.

And I need to accept my life as it is. No matter how much it sucks.

TEN

Olivia

I know I'm not supposed to like Mondays, but I secretly love them. They're a fresh start, another chance to get life right, all recharged and ready to go. But this Monday, I wish I could go back and re-do my weekend, call in sick to community service, and avoid spending an entire day aching to touch Jace.

Or, better yet, turn back time even farther and stop myself from kissing him behind the bakery in the first place and making a strained situation even strainier.

My angst is affecting Princess too, which is why, instead of heading home Monday night after my last tour at the factory, I tuck my hedgehog into my sidecar and point my Vespa toward the animal sanctuary.

Poor Hope was having such a hard time on Saturday. And maybe being out here with the animals when Jace isn't around will help clear my head. I've got to do something, before I turn into one of those people who wander around in a haze, longing for things that will never be, wasting my life wishing when I could be dreaming.

Dreams have a chance of coming true, if you work hard and believe even harder. But until genies become a real thing, wishes are just a waste of your soul fire.

Princess von Spooksalot and I park in the mostly empty lot and head toward the office. Just as we reach the steps, Hope slams out of the building with a scowl. "Oh, yes, because I *wanted* everything to break. Asshole," she mutters.

"Um, hi?" I say.

She startles and glances over, laughing as her cheeks go pink. "Olivia! Sorry. I didn't see you there."

"Is everything okay?"

"Yes. No." She winces, letting out a long breath. "Yes. It will be. I just have to get over being a freak."

"You're not a freak!" I object with a sneeze that makes Princess huff in surprise. Though, really, she ought to be getting used to it by now. Sneezing has become my second full-time job and none of the allergy remedies are working.

"No, I am a freak. It's all right. I can handle the truth." She shakes her head. "Walk with me? I need to check on Chewpaca. He's still adjusting to his new pen. And since he's not a toaster oven, I should be able to get close to him without anything exploding." She winks. "Plus, I think he misses you."

I laugh. "I miss him too. Even if he is a pervert."

"He learned it from watching Princess," she teases, leaning down to the hedgehog's level as she adds, "Isn't that right, trouble? How's it going?"

Princess starts to purr—something I had no idea hedgehogs could even do until she shoplifted her security panties—and I roll my eyes. "Oh, it's going. Still humping stuffed squirrels and waving her panties in the air like she just don't care."

Hope chuckles again as we fall into step together on the way out to the pasture.

"And seriously, you're not a freak," I insist, not ready to let that go without a fight. People do so much damage with their words, to each other, yes, but mostly, I've found, to themselves. "You're a Wiper. You've got a naturally dangerous energy field. You were probably born that way, but there are absolutely things you can do to calm it down."

"Really? Like what, if you don't mind me asking. Because I'm getting pretty desperate over here." She thrusts her fingers through her short hair. "If I break another computer, I'm going to have to start selling kittens instead of giving them away to pay for a new one. Ginger suggested selling the Persian ones the other day when she was helping me scoop out the litter boxes while she waited for Jace. But I hate to charge for anything except shots and meds, you know?"

I think I succeed in not wincing when she says Ginger's name, but I'm not completely sure, so I glance over at the pasture and pretend the sun's in my eyes. "I totally get it. And as far as what might help your situation, exercise is good for some people. Though, in others, it can make things worse in the long run, by boosting your overall health and vitality."

"I'm pretty sure it makes mine worse. I've been running a lot lately and it's explosion city over here."

I nod sympathetically. "I heard about the lawn mower. And the pinball machine."

"But I don't want to stop exercising..." She peeks at me from the corner of her eyes. "I've kind of been hoping to get in good enough shape to run a half marathon. My cousins all say I'm crazy, but I think I could do it."

"You can totally do it!" I enthuse. "You're in amazing shape. I've seen you, Hope. You work everyone else into the ground. And you're right, you shouldn't stop exercising. Not at all." I smile. "You just need to have more sex."

She laughs, a little uncomfortably. "Sex?"

"Yes. Sex. It's the ultimate energy release and a great chakra-balancer. Orgasms release excess electrical charge and the resulting afterglow will give you better control over what you have left."

"Oh. Well…okay then." She's eyeing me dubiously, but that's not unusual. "More sex. I'll add that to the list. Thanks, Olivia. It's nice to have someone around who doesn't think I'm crazy.

"Of course, I don't! And ditto." I nudge her shoulder with mine. "A lot of people around here think I'm a little out there too. We woo-woo girls have to stick together."

"We do." We reach the new fence that Jace finished on Saturday—*oh, Jace*—and she smiles and bends over to stroke Princess. "So let's talk more about our girl. I've been doing some research on hedgehog behavior and I think Princess is self-anointing with the panties. It's a process where the hedgehog chews on an object they find to have a particularly pleasing smell, creating a foamy saliva that they then spread all over their quills."

I nod. "I read about self-anointing, but I didn't know if it was normal to do that with…human panties. I mean, I would have taken them away from her, but they seem to give her comfort. And at least they're clean panties."

Hope grins. "Yeah, it's totally fine. No one's really sure why they self-anoint. It could be for camouflage in a new environment. Or maybe just because they dig a certain smell and want to keep it around."

"Like hedgehog perfume?" I ask.

She points her finger gun my way and pulls the trigger.

"Exactly. But it's all good. She's just doing what hedgehogs do."

What a relief. I rest a hand on my chest. "So I'm not a terrible hedgehog mama?"

"Not at all," she assures me as an alpaca with a heart of cotton candy and sprinkles comes skipping toward us from the other side of the wide enclosure at the corner of the pasture. "And look at how far she's come since you adopted her. She hardly spooks at all anymore."

"I should change her name to von Humpsalot," I say, laughing even as my forehead furrows. "So the squirrel humping is normal too?"

She hesitates. "Um…well, not *quite* as normal, no. I mean, males seem to hump things all the time, but it's more unusual in females. Females tend to be more passive and can even be raised together in captivity, which experts don't recommend with males."

Hm. That's not quite as reassuring, but… "Maybe Princess is just embracing her woman power? Trying to even the humping field."

"Well, someone should," she says with a smile and a shrug. "It's not fair that men have all the fun."

"Well, not *all* the fun…" I murmur before I can stop myself. Even though I'm not supposed to be thinking about fun or men or all the fun I had with one particular man.

Her brows shoot up. "What! You've actually found someone decent to date around here?! Do tell, because in my experience, all the good guys are already taken. All that's left are jerks who think you're a borderline psychotic who enjoys breaking electronics on purpose."

"Oh, no, I don't mean anyone specific," I lie. And then I sneeze, and Princess huffs, and Chewpaca is suddenly there, leaning over the fence, trying to lick my face. I reach up, stroking the soft fur on his neck, while I shift so

Princess is safe from his affections. "Well, hey there, you handsome fella."

Chewpaca moo-moans and sticks his tongue in my ear.

"Whoa, back up there, Chewy." Hope gets between us, laughing. "Sorry. He's not usually *this* affectionate."

I narrow my eyes. "He must sense a disturbance in the force."

She laughs, and I give my devoted Romeo one final pat before stepping back and reaching into the sling to assure myself Princess is still okay. She rubs her little face against my thumb and bats at my bracelets, like a normal, healthy hedgehog.

She *is* a normal, healthy hedgehog. She's just a little odd sometimes, but aren't we all? I like to eat mustard on my cauliflower and bathe in moonlight; she enjoys drowning spiders in her water bowl and has a slightly more robust sex drive than the average female hedgehog.

We all just need to live and let live and fly our freak flags high!

As if summoned by my freak flag thoughts, a sheriff's car carrying a man with his own unique aura pulls into the parking lot just as Hope, Princess, and I amble back onto the lawn by the house.

"Well, well, hello there, ladies," Chester says, swaggering across the gravel, his thumbs hooked in his gun belt.

Hope winces, and I have to work to find my smile. But I do, because we're all at our own place in the journey of life and it's really not Chester's fault that his aura makes mine shudder like it just smelled moldy carrots. "Hello, deputy," I say politely.

He beams at me. "Hey there, Miss Moonbeam. Aren't you lookin' prettier than a peach in a cornfield today."

I don't understand what that means, but I keep smiling anyway. "And you're looking very official."

"What can we help you with, Chester?" Hope asks, her all-business tone urging him to get to the point.

He hitches his uniform pants up and smiles broadly at me with spinach stuck between his two front teeth. "Just checking in. You're not here for more hours, are you, Livie? Seems wrong, giving you that much community service for your religious beliefs."

"Um, thank you," I say. "But I guess I was technically breaking the law. And community service brought me to Hope and Chewpaca and the dogs, so everything turned out beautifully in the end."

He winks. I think. Either that, or his eye has a seizure. "Well, if you ever want to go moon-bathing again, you let me know, and I'll make sure you're not disturbed, if you get my drift."

Hope makes a gagging sound that turns into a rush of words. "Oh my gosh, Olivia, I am *so sorry* to ask you this, but do you have a tampon? I completely forgot to go to the store this weekend and I am bleeding hard. Sooooo hard. You know how it is? When your vagina decides to try to murder you a little?"

Before I can assure her that I have an organic tampon — or suggest to her that she give a menstrual cup a try because they're so easy to use and environmentally friendly — Chester makes his own gagging sound.

His face beet red, he tips his hat and backs away. "All right, then. Well, you ladies have a lovely afternoon. Livie, you call me if you need anything."

"He's such a creepy dude," she mutters as he folds himself into his car and pulls out. "I know it's not his fault — his mom used to run a circus school and clown college and was always making Chester dress up as Woopsy the Sad Clown for town carnivals and shit. And he wasn't a cute clown. Plus, after the tornado wiped out part of the school, she left him here with his weird aunt to go set up a new school somewhere else and never came back."

"That's really sad," I say softly, because I know what it's like to not have a mom. But at least I had her until I was a teenager. And she didn't abandon me.

"It is, and I know I should be more sympathetic." She shivers. "But he just gets to me, you know? Hanging around all the time and butting in where he's not welcome and skeeving all over everything in a skirt. He's been drooling down Ginger's cleavage since they were kids, apparently. Or so she said."

Ginger. There she is again. I can't get away from her, or Jace, no matter how hard I try. "Well, I think he's just trying to do his job," I say, in an attempt to be fair.

"Incompetently. He didn't want you to have community service for exposing your breasts, but he's out here heckling Jace for taking a leak behind a trash can? Is there really such a big difference between the two?"

I frown, because I hadn't thought about that, and I should've. "You're right. That's not fair."

"It's really not. I mean, I know Jace is no angel, but—"

"He's a good man," I cut in, leaping to his defense before I can stop myself. I clear my throat, trying to play it cool as I add. "I mean, he seems good. And kind. And very thoughtful, even though most people don't give him credit for it."

Chewpaca moos plaintively in the distance. Or groans. Or whatever it is that alpacas do. Princess huffs knowingly, and Hope shoots a curious look my way.

"I just don't think anyone should be called good or bad based on a few moments in their life," I add softly. And then I sneeze. Hard.

She smiles. "You make a very good point. Complete

with sneeze punctuation. Do you have dinner plans? I hate eating alone every night."

"I love dinner dates," I say. "They're so much less lonely. And I'm not just saying that because you're my community service warden."

She laughs again. "Me too. Come on. I've got everything we need for summer stir-fry."

I wave goodbye to Chewpaca, and my sweet hedgehog and I head into the office and on into the home's cozy kitchen with Hope. I can still feel Jace's energy haunting the fence posts, but I'm well on my way to making new, girlfriends-only memories here now.

Baby steps. But I'll get there. Someday I'll walk by that fence and not think of the one who got away. Someday I'll realize I was wrong about my Kindred Penis.

Someday I'll have finally let Jace go.

ELEVEN

Jace

It's Tuesday—late—but I'm ignoring the clock, doing a deep clean after karaoke night at the Wild Hedgehog.

Shit. The Wild *Hog*. Not Hedgehog.

I have got to get Olivia off my brain. So far, cleaning everything isn't doing it, but still, I'm cleaning *everything*. The karaoke stage. The floor. The chairs.

The gum under the tables.

The bottoms of the trash cans.

That space between the tap pulls that I have to use a toothbrush to get to.

And it's not all related to Olivia.

"You expecting the health department?" Blake asks.

"Yeah," I mumble. "Let's go with that. Get your elbow off the bar. I just cleaned it."

"My elbows aren't dirty."

I sigh. "They can still smear shit."

"My elbows are fine and I'm going to put them where I want to put them, dammit."

"Fine. Jesus." I shoot him a narrow look, but don't comment on his bad attitude. He spent most of the night rescuing Hope after her truck broke down in the boonies somewhere, and is apparently pissed about it.

I've never understood what's up with those two—and I'm still committed to *not remembering* that shit I saw on Saturday—but then, my brothers have never understood me and Ginger either. Love and hate are equally mysterious.

Still, he gets paid time and a half for fix-it calls after eight, so he shouldn't be bitching. He didn't complain about fixing Maud and Gerald's air conditioner at three AM last week, and Gerald is a pain in the ass even when he hasn't woken up in a sweat in the middle of the night. And if Blake didn't bait Hope, she wouldn't be cranky either.

Not that I'm one to talk about being cranky. Or weird...

I'm not getting paid anything extra to spiff up my bar for a clientele that won't notice. I am, however, avoiding going to Ginger's place.

He sighs, adding a second elbow to my clean bar and plunking his chin on his fists. "You talk to Olivia lately?"

My shoulders twitch. "Can't remember."

"You *can't remember*? The last time I talked to Goddess Core, she offered to realign my chakras. That's not the sort of thing a normal guy forgets."

"Afraid of a little woo-woo?" I ask. "And quit calling her that. The lipstick joke is old." So Olivia has a lipstick that's Goddess Core pink and isn't embarrassed to talk about it, so what? It's no reason to mock her for the rest of her life in Happy Cat.

"I wasn't making fun of her, dude. Relax. I'm just saying

she's memorable, that's all. Most people from Happy Cat don't talk the way she does. She's different."

"Different doesn't mean *wrong*."

He grunts. "Yeah. Got it. And agreed. I'm open to the woo-woo, man. I actually asked her to drop by the house and give me some pointers on biodynamic farming methods for my grapes. Apparently, if you fill a ram's horn with compost and bury it on the full moon it increases fruit yield."

"Awesome," I mutter, because he's growing his grapes right next to my house. So he's bringing Olivia and a fucking ram's horn filled with shit practically to my front door.

Olivia, who's been in my dreams every single night since that kiss, who I've been fighting like hell *not* to think about during the day, whose ghost is haunting the floor I'm standing on. Can live people have ghosts? Because I swear there's a part of her still in the bar. Sometimes I see her out of the corner of my eye, lying naked in a shaft of moonlight, looking so gorgeous it just about rips my heart out of my chest.

And there she is again. Dancing naked through my thoughts, right when I was starting to forget her. Or at least, not remember too intensely. Until my bonehead brother had to bring her up. "Bonehead," I mutter beneath my breath, though apparently not too softly for Blake to hear.

"Dude. What is up with you?" He frowns.

"Just tired of your cranky ass, I guess," I say, doubling down as his eyebrows shoot up. "That's right. You, Mr. Ram's Horn. Now, you gonna help me get out of here some-time tonight, or you gonna sit there and gossip? Last time I checked, arcade games don't clean themselves."

He takes the rag I toss his way, but he doesn't head for

the arcade games in the back room. Instead, he leans his elbows on my bar again. "So…do you think you and Ginger should see a counselor or something? I'm assuming that's why you're biting my head off right now?"

"We're fine. She's in Atlanta, doing some baby shopping with her mom." And she's actually been extra sweet lately. Hasn't complained about the long hours I've been working, laughed it off when I finally confessed I can't stand bologna, and texted to say that she missed me and was coming home early so I should stop by tonight to feel how much her breasts have already grown.

The message came accompanied by a picture of Ginger's ample and objectively appetizing cleavage, but despite the view that used to rev my engines, my pants pickle refused to wake up and smell the sex vibes.

I need to talk to her. I've *needed* to talk to her, but guilt keeps getting in the way. But it's time to be honest. Ask if we can be good friends who raise the baby together, but nothing more. That's a thing. People do it. I honestly think Ginger and I are better off as friends.

And I *know* I'd be a much less cranky bastard with Olivia in my future. Even *a shot* with her would make me feel like I'd won the lottery. Even if I fuck it up—the way I do most things—at least I won't be haunted by the ghosts of "what could've been" for the rest of my life.

Too bad I also know Ginger well enough to realize that being "just friends" will go over like a fart in church.

Blake's watching me. He has our mom's green gaze, and it doesn't help to see Mom's eyes staring me down across the bar when my life is spinning out of control.

How many times did I let her down when I was growing up?

Baseballs through the window. Detentions for fighting at school. Sneaking out to drink and party in the MacIntoshes' cornfields and getting caught dirt biking in the nature preserve.

Knocking up a woman I can't honestly say I'm in love with.

"Look, if you need—" he starts, but the front door bangs open, and Ginger strolls in.

"Whoops," she says as she pulls it closed behind her. "Wind must've caught it. Hello, Blake. Hey, baby."

She's in a skin-tight denim skirt that barely covers her ass and a ruffled green shirt that's loose at the waist. Her curly red hair is wild tonight, teased out in that way that used to drive me crazy with the need to thrust my fingers through it and add my mark, to claim that bedhead was *mine*.

But there's still no action happening south of my belt.

No *good* action. It's all recoil and take cover.

I've got to do something.

I have to tell her the way I really feel.

"That's my cue," Blake announces. "Y'all have a good one."

He leaves his rag on the bar and heads out, nodding to Ginger as he passes.

She smiles back. It's the same flirty grin she was beaming up at Bart Tompkins three months ago, the night they played beer pong on my karaoke stage and then left together.

We just went to play pool, she insisted later. *Your table was all booked up and I wanted to play.*

I told her she should've said so, and I would've kicked off whoever was on my table. But she'd called me jealous, said it made her hot when I got possessive, and then given me a blow job that'd convinced me we needed a Mexican make-up-sex getaway, just the two of us.

Because that's how we've always been. She flirts, I get jealous, we fight, we make up.

For years.

And now here we are with the results of that trip binding us together for life, and the only reason I'm considering being pissed that she gave my brother that sexy smile is because I don't want him getting sucked into the fucked-up mess my love life has become.

She swings her hips, taking her time strolling up to the bar, and I watch. I can't help it. She says it's too soon to see the baby bump, but I keep looking for it anyway. It would be nice to have a visual reminder of why I have to keep fighting for peace and harmony. I *do* want to know my baby.

I want to feel her kick. I want to know that she can hear my voice, and I can't wait to hear her say *dada* for the first time.

"You're working so late," Ginger says in her breathless kitten voice. "I missed you."

"Health inspection soon," I say. In a month, probably, but it's all I can come up with.

She fiddles with the strap on her shirt, sliding it off her shoulder. "But it's not tonight, is it, baby?"

I shake my head, wondering if a Ginger striptease special might finally wake things up in Dickville, but there's still zero signs of life down there.

"So we could have some fun," she continues, drawing the strap farther down, exposing the top of one breast. "I've always wanted to do it on the pool table, haven't you?"

Still nothing. My cock might as well have left the building.

"You know Chester has it in for me," I say, voice tight. "Put your shirt back on before someone looks in and we get arrested."

"We could lock the door," she says, with a giggle.

"But we can't cover all the windows." I'm sweating now. My upper lip, between my shoulders, under my balls, making me wonder if ball sweat would be a good enough excuse to bow out of pool table sex. If not, I could always fake a stomach bug.

"Oh, come on, Jacey," she wheedles, biting her bottom lip. "We used to do it *everywhere*. Remember the barn? When we were kids? The first time I sucked your cock and made you come?"

"Ginger. Not here."

She reaches the bar and leans toward me, shimmying her shirt lower until her nipples are almost showing, and pressing her breasts together to display a motherload of cleavage. "But don't you want to lick me, Jacey? I want to lick you."

She goes up on her toes to lean in for a kiss, just like Olivia did the night we got hammered on Dr. Peppy, and I'm looking at Ginger and her red curls and green eyes, but seeing Olivia's happy face and dangly bracelets.

This isn't right and it's never going to be.

I push back before her lips touch mine. "We need to talk."

She goes as still as a jungle cat. "That again?"

I swallow hard, because I don't want to hurt her. She's been in my life since high school, and, as the mother of my child, she'll always be a part of my life. But— "I don't know if I can do this," I confess.

"Do. What?"

She's still not moving, but danger hangs heavy between us. I'll take it as a good sign that she hasn't cried yet, like she did the last time I tried this, but I still need to choose my words carefully.

My ass connects with the cabinets against the wall and I

lift my hands in surrender. "Ginger. Listen. You know you're important to me. We've been together for a long time. I want to do right by you, and I want to do right by the baby, but I just...I'm not..." *Fuck*, this is hard.

"Don't do this," she breathes, and I know I need to shut up and nod along and not screw this up too, but what's better—living a lie, or finding a real solution?

"I'm not abandoning you," I tell her. "I'm not leaving you. Or the baby. I'm going to take care of you both. But I... I'm not in love with you anymore."

Pain flashes over her features, and I flinch.

"I'm sorry. I don't want to hurt you," I start, but she cuts me off.

"Take it back."

"Swear to god, Ginger, I would if I could, but I *can't*. I'm trying. I'm trying my heart out here, but—"

"Try. Harder." Her eyes glitter with unshed tears, making me feel even worse.

"Ginger." I silently beg her to understand, because I don't think she loves me either. Does she? "Some things you just can't fake."

"Why are you *doing* this to me? To me *and our baby*?"

Guilt claws at my stomach. "I'm just trying to find a way for everyone to be happy."

"You don't want us." Her bottom lip quivers.

"No! Yes! Ginger, *yes*, I want you and the baby both in my life. I want us to work together and give this kid everything, but I don't—"

"But secretly you think you'd be better off without us?" Her voice is getting quieter and quieter, the way it does when I've really pissed her off, making the hairs on the back of my neck stand at attention. "So I should just get rid of the baby, and then you can get rid of me? Is *that* what you want?"

My entire body flushes. "No. *No.* Ginger, I want this baby. And I'm going to take care of you both, and I—"

"Then let's get married."

I exhale in a rush. "No."

"Yes," she insists, swiping tears from her cheeks with her fists. "You promised you were going to marry me. You promised!"

"I never—"

"Maybe not in words, but you said it in other ways," she says, her brows drawing together. "You know you did. So marry me, Jace, and let's be happy together. Or I swear to god, you will *never* see me *or* this baby. *Ever again.*"

"Ginger—"

"I'll move away!" Her voice rises. "I'll move, and I'll change my name, and you'll never even know if I had a boy or a girl. Or *twins.* Is that what you want, Jace? You want me to disappear and take your baby? Because if you won't marry me, why should I stay here? To be embarrassed in front of the entire community? To have the parents of my students look at me like some whore who got used up and thrown away?"

My throat tightens.

"To stay," she says, eyes shining again, "and listen to my friends tell me every day that I should have known better than to get pregnant by the town screw-up?"

I'm rooted to the spot. My heart's trying to jackhammer its way through my stomach. I'm dripping in cold sweat, and I can't remember the last time I ate, but I'm fairly certain I'm going to throw up.

Because she's right. I can't do that to her. I can't drag her down to my level. I can't make her a joke or our baby the punch line. I have to suck it the hell up and do the right thing.

"Okay." My throat is so tight it hurts to speak, but I force the words out. "Okay. You're right."

"Really?" She blinks, as if she's surprised I'm doing the right thing, a fact that makes my chest ache and me even more determined to prove I'm not a waste of human flesh.

I reach out, taking her hand. "Really. We'll get married. Okay? We'll do what's right by our kid, give him or her a real shot in this town."

In a heartbeat, her face transforms, sadness vanishing as she lifts a hand to her cheek. "Oh my god, Jace, *I'm so happy!* We're getting married! Oh my god. *Oh my god.* Thank you, baby. Thank you so much." She wraps her arms tight around my neck and a part of me is almost happy about it.

This is hard as hell, but no one ever said being a good man was going to be easy.

She kisses my cheek. "You're the best and I love you so much." She pulls back with a sniff and another big smile. "I'm going to go call my mom, okay? She was so worried about me, what with us not having set a date or anything, but now she'll be thrilled!"

Thrilled. Yeah. That's good. Someone should be. Weddings are supposed to be exciting things. I don't know if I can get there myself, but I'm going to do my best not to rain on Ginger or her mom's parade.

I force a smile. "I'll close up and come with you. We can call her together."

She beams, threading her fingers slowly through mine. "That sounds perfect. And don't worry, babe. We're going to fall in love again. I promise. We just need a little time to find our way, but you know us. We always do."

I nod. "We do."

And she's right, we always have.

Deep down, I know this time is different, *I'm* different,

but only a heartless bastard would tell his pregnant fiancée that he's in love with someone else. And I'm not going to be a bastard this time. I'm going to be the good guy, the one my kid will be proud to call his or her father.

This is my life.

This is my life, and I'm going to make the best of it, even if Olivia's ghost haunts me for the rest of my days.

TWELVE

Olivia

I can't stop sneezing. I am a sneeze machine, creating sneezes at such a relentless pace that I get sent home early from work on Thursday. Cassie shows up in the afternoon with a pot of fresh vegetable soup from the Kennedy Family Day School, which used to be a real school but is now an adorable sandwich shop near my favorite path through the woods around Happy Cat.

She's so sweet to think of me. And the soup is delicious, though I feel a little guilty eating it.

I don't feel sick and I've been taking teaspoons of every kind of honey sold locally to help combat allergies, but nothing's working to stop the sneezing.

"I hate to say it, but maybe it's Princess?" Cassie says as she and George settle on my couch, Cassie with a to-go cup of coffee, George with a bag full of popcorn.

I stroke my hedgehog's quills as she sniffs at the air. I made her a playground in a box. She loves the running wheel, tunnels, and slide, but so far, she's struggled to appreciate the seesaw, which is understandable. It's really a two-hedgehog operation. She needs a playmate.

Other than me.

And Sir Pendleton.

"Hedgehogs don't carry dander," I say. "And if I were allergic, her quills would make my skin break ou—ou—*achoo!*"

Her forehead furrows in sympathy. "Aw, you poor thing."

I'm beginning to suspect exactly why I'm sneezing.

It's because I have a secret. This is my body's way of telling me that I can't keep it all bottled up anymore. I need to let it go. Otherwise, the more I hold it in, the more my body will keep trying to expel it.

Only keep a secret if the secret isn't keeping you, my mom used to say.

"Oh my gosh, is that Sir Pendleton?" Cassie rises, heading to my bookshelf where the squirrel is watching all of us.

His moustache seems extra judgy today. Like he disapproves of secrets too, which makes sense, him being an Investigator at Large and all. Investigators are in the business of unearthing secrets, bringing them out into the light where they shrivel back down to a manageable size and can't eat anyone alive anymore.

She pulls Sir down and frowns at him. "This isn't one of Gordon's creations is it?"

"I didn't ask," I confess. I know Gordon, but we have a fundamental disagreement over taxidermied animals. So even though I see him every time I go to the post office—his shop is in the same building—we don't talk much. "George pulled him out of the trash the night that—" I stop myself. This secret is a curse upon my soul and nose, but *no good will come of Cassie knowing*.

She's dating Jace's brother. She'll tell Ryan, and then Ryan will talk to Jace, and then the secret will impact everyone here who's become my family.

I sneeze again.

I could tell Hope, except that I don't know her well enough to guess how good she is at keeping secrets. And she's connected to people who shouldn't be told about this either. Like Blake, who, due to her energy field, spends an inordinate amount of time at her place fixing things.

"Gordon's squirrels are all superheroes, not at all proper and Sherlock Holmes-ish," she muses. "Sir Pendleton is adorable though, isn't he, George?"

George shrinks back on the couch and throws a popcorn kernel at Sir Pendleton, whose glassy eyes stare disapprovingly at the trash panda.

"George!" Cassie exclaims. "It's not nice to throw popcorn in other people's houses. Okay, really, in Ryan's house either, but especially not when we're company."

She sets Sir Pendleton on my mom's old wine barrel end table, and George dives for the ground, popcorn bag in hand, spilling it everywhere before waddling behind my armchair.

"He is so weird sometimes," she says. "Sorry, I'll clean that up."

"Don't worry about it. And he's probably freaked out because Sir Pendleton's haunted. Didn't you see his moustache move?"

She glances at me, then at the squirrel, and laughs. "No. But ten points for making me look."

I laugh too, even though the crazier part of me feels like Sir Pendleton *does* have a strange energy field all of his own. Which is odd for a dearly departed creature. But I'm not going to tell Cassie *that* secret, either.

I sneeze three more times, and she makes a clucking noise and strokes my hair while Princess crawls over to sit in her lap. Because Cassie's *not* sneezing, and laps without sneezes attached are preferable in all respects.

"Have you called your doctor? I know you don't like traditional medicine, but sweetie, sometimes it really helps."

"No, this will pass." I'm certain it will. As soon as I confide in someone about what happened with Jace.

That's what I need to do. Once I put the secret out there —into the ears of the right person, someone who won't tell *anyone* or be directly affected by the secret in any way, then I'll stop sneezing.

But I don't know where I'm going to find someone in a town this size who isn't connected to the O'Dells or Ginger in some form or fashion, which means—

"*Achoo! Achoo achoo!*"

Princess snuffles at me from Cassie's lap, where she's trying to nibble the button off of Cassie's hot pink shorts. "Princess! We talked about this," I say softly. "You can love people without *loving* them."

Cassie just laughs and pulls her away.

"I'm sorry," I say. "Maud's panties started fraying so badly I was afraid she was going to choke on them so I took them away. Now she keeps trying to steal mine, but I learned my lesson and don't let her help me fold laundry anymore."

"I love you, you know that?" she says, and I blush, because I don't feel worthy of love.

Not with the secret I'm keeping.

Maybe I should tell Princess.

Maybe she knows I'm not confiding in her, and that's why she's obsessed with panties. Because she knows I have a panty secret and no one likes a panty secret.

Sir Pendleton watches me with judgy eyes. *You need to tell a person, not a hedgehog. Only a person can talk you through this*, he says in his proper British accent.

Okay, yes, I *imagine* that he says that, because stuffed inspector squirrels can't talk.

But still, he's probably right. I *have* to tell someone. I have to get this off my chest and nose before I go even crazier than I am already.

It's coming. I can feel it rising, rising, before it bursts from my lips with the force of a super-powered sneeze. "I had sex with Jace!" I blurt out before I can stop myself.

Cassie's eyes go saucer wide. "Whoa. Did *not* see that one coming."

"It was before we knew Ginger was pregnant," I ramble, all of it spilling out now that I've started. "They were broken up. And we had this incredible connection, and I felt so close to him, and I was sure I'd found my Kindred Penis. And he's *such* a good guy, Cassie, truly, even though I know most people can't see it. And I know he cared about me—maybe even still cares about me—and I just want to be with him and care about him too. But he has to be with—with—with—*achoooo!*" I bring my hands to cover my face, peeking between my spread fingers. "With Ginger. Not me."

"Oh, Olivia," she whispers.

George peers out from behind the armchair, popping popcorn into his mouth like he's enjoying the show before pausing to throw another kernel at Sir Pendleton.

"I know," I whisper back. "I was weak. I hadn't been with anyone since Baxter. Do you remember him? The guy who said the spirits moved him to come to Happy Cat to find true love, except he was really just looking for a new place to plant marijuana since his operation was shut down in Cobb County?"

"I don't think I was here then, but I remember Savannah telling me he put your name on the permit for his processing shed. Since he had a prior conviction for dealing."

I sniff. "Yeah, he was a user, not a lover. Which is sad, because marijuana *can* really help people who need it."

"That was a while ago," she says quietly. "And it sounds like this thing with Jace was a lot more intense than your fling with Baxter."

My lips turn down. "It was. It was just one night, but... it really was. And I know I should forget it ever happened because Ginger and the baby need him, and I just *want* him." I shake my head. "And I'm trying not to want him, I really am. I'm trying so hard."

"Oh, honey, I'm so sorry." She pulls me into a hug that reminds me of the hugs my mom used to give, before she got sick, when she could still wrap me up and hold on tight, so I squeeze my eyes shut and concentrate on breathing.

Good air in, secrets out.

And then my nose tickles, and I barely manage to pull back before I sneeze all over Cassie, Princess, and Sir Pendleton.

And I sneeze.

And sneeze.

And sneeze.

"Oh, honey," she says again, passing me the box of tissues.

"It's okay," I tell her. "Just clearing out the residual parts of my secret. Now that it's out I should stop sneezing."

She gives me the usual *I don't think that's how it works, but I love you anyway* look, and I don't judge her for it. Her mind works in numbers and computer code, not in the ethereal connection of our spirits to the earth, and that's okay. The world needs all of us with all of our various talents and gifts.

George suddenly bolts out from behind the chair, chittering up a storm and throwing more popcorn as he hops on three legs down the hall, still clutching his bag.

"*George!*" Cassie exclaims as I realize what the problem is.

"*Princess von Spooksalot!*"

I dive across Cassie to grab my hedgehog from the top of the wine barrel table. She's up on her hind legs again, front paws holding tight to Sir Pendleton's tail as she thrusts her hips against his thick base fur. "No, no, sweet girl, we don't chase squirrel tail!"

She's still pumping her pelvis as I pry her off Sir Pendleton, who's definitely wearing his hat at a very disapproving angle now.

"Sorry," I whisper to him. "She loves who she loves."

"Oh my God, I'm sorry," Cassie wheezes, laughing so hard she can barely breathe. "I didn't think you were serious about the squirrel humping."

"Princess, we need to find you a better companion. A *live* one. A very understanding, patient, *live* companion."

She huffs indignantly, and a giggling Cassie snaps a picture of the two of us. "You two are quite the pair. And I feel another hedgehog shaming photo coming on."

I sneeze.

And then sneeze again.

"It didn't work," I say, cursing beneath my breath. "I'm still sneezing, even with my secret out and about, squirming through another person's brain."

"Olivia," she says gently, "I don't think it's my brain you needed to tell. You need to tell Jace how you feel."

I blink, shocked at the thought. "But he's with Ginger. She's having his child."

"Yeah, she is, but the baby wasn't planned and…" She shrugs, lifting her hands to face the ceiling. "And the world isn't black and white. And *with Ginger* may not be completely accurate." She wrinkles her nose. "Those two are…"

"Not soulmates," I whisper.

"Yeah. Let's go with that." Her tone makes me think maybe she isn't as much of a Ginger fan as the rest of the town. "And just because Ginger's pregnant doesn't mean Jace has to live unhappily ever after with her. He can be a good father *and* also be crazy about you. How lucky would the baby be to have *three* adults—plus all of the O'Dells—who love him or her with their whole heart? It's not about fighting, right? It's about finding a way to get along and let love win."

I stare at her. "You sound like Savannah."

"Who would say she was channeling *you* if she gave me that lecture."

I set Princess in her playground box and step around Cassie to fix Sir Pendleton's tail and put him out of reach again.

"Love isn't something to be ashamed of or kept secret, Olivia," Cassie says softly. "Just tell him how you feel. Before they get married on Saturday, preferably."

I spin, heart jerking hard in my chest. "What?"

She blinks. "They're getting married. On Saturday. Didn't you hear? It's all over the town InstaChat page."

"I don't go there. InstaChat makes me feel lonely," I say, my voice thin.

"Aw, why's that?" she asks, cocking her head sympathetically to the side.

"Because I can't feel people's auras through a computer. And I want to. I want a true connection, to know how they really feel," I say, struggling to breathe. It's getting harder and harder to convince my ribs to expand. I mean, I knew that Jace and Ginger were trying to make it work as a couple, but "as a couple" and "married on Saturday" are two totally different things. The thought makes panicked words fly from my mouth. "Jace isn't ready for this, Cassie. They can't get married. It will be a disaster. I just know it."

She places a gentle hand on my shoulder. "I agree. But it hasn't happened yet. It's not too late to turn it all around. I know Jace wants to do the right thing but that doesn't have to include a wedding. Maybe you can get through to him about that, huh? You're good at getting through to people."

She's right.

And what baby *wouldn't* be lucky to have more people who loved him or her?

And I would. I'd love Jace's baby with my whole heart.

I smile at Cassie, and then I sneeze again.

"And seriously, *see your doctor* about that." Her phone dings, and she smiles. "You okay if I dash? Ryan got off a double shift this morning and has been sleeping all day. We haven't really seen each other since Monday night."

"Go." I shoo her off with my hands. "And thank you for the soup. And for listening. And please don't—"

"Tell anybody." She nods, eyes widening meaningfully. "Of course not. This is between you and Jace. Just let me know if you need an ear again, okay?"

"You're the best soul sister in the entire world." I hug her tight.

"You're pretty stinking awesome yourself," she says, returning the embrace.

And when she leaves, I'm still sneezing, but I'm not down.

Because she's right.

It's not too late to turn this around or to tell Jace everything that's in my heart.

THIRTEEN

Olivia

For the past few weeks, I've seen Jace everywhere I go. No matter how hard I've tried to avoid him or to deny the feelings that rise inside me every time our eyes meet, he's always right there, looking sexy and sweet and tormented by twists of fate beyond our control.

But maybe they're *not* beyond our control.

Maybe it's not too late to find out if every night together would be as magical as our first night.

If I can just find him, dang it…

Of course, now that I'm actually *looking* for the most gorgeous bartender in town, he's nowhere to be found. I try the bar first, but his bar back, Poppy, is manning the taps tonight and has no idea where Jace is.

"He said he had a thing," she says, wrinkling her regal nose, the one that makes her look more like a French queen than a farm girl. "Something at the fire station, maybe? With his brother? But don't quote me."

I thank her and hurry out into the fading light.

It's after eight, but the sky is still rosy and kids are running wild on the square, throwing Frisbees and bouncing balls and hanging on their parents' legs, begging for five more minutes before heading home to bed. I pass a little girl with blond curls and a chocolate ice cream moustache explaining to her daddy in a serious voice that "when you're four you get to stay up later than the sun, those are the rules," and hide a smile behind my hand.

She's adorable and it's so easy to imagine Jace's daughter being every bit as sassy and clever. Though she'll probably have brown hair, like her daddy. Or maybe red, like her mom, which will be beautiful.

Ginger's a beautiful woman, she's just not the woman for Jace. And deep in her heart, I'm betting she knows that. She's probably just scared of raising a baby alone or worried what the people in town will think of her for having a child outside of wedlock. Happy Cat is a small, old-fashioned town. Things like that are still a big deal around here. I realize that now, though I admit it took me a while.

Back in California, I knew tons of women having babies solo. My own mother had me on her own twenty-four years ago and no one raised an eyebrow, even way back then.

But things are different here, a fact I'm reminded of as I pause outside the women's health center a couple blocks from the factory, waiting for the people exiting the building to make their way down the sidewalk toward their cars. A birthing class must have just let out because all of the people are coupled up and each of the smiling women is sporting a baby bump.

They're all so beautiful, their auras shimmering with the

promise of life and hope and the miracle of bringing a much-anticipated new person into the world, that I can't help but get a little choked up. And sneezy...

I tug my handkerchief from my purse just in time to cover my nose as another sneeze attack hits with a vengeance. A few of the mothers-to-be cast nervous glances in my direction and shift onto the grass beside the sidewalk, clearly wanting no part of my germs.

I want to assure them that I'm not sick, but that would involve talking, which is hard to do when you Can't.

Stop.

Sneezing.

"Give me a break already, nose. I'm trying, okay?" I sag down onto the steps of the building beside the health center to recover and wait until the pregnant parade has passed. I have to find Jace before this sneeze situation gets any worse.

But I can see the firehouse from here, and things look pretty quiet over there. And now that I think about it, I remember Cassie said Ryan wasn't going to be at the station tonight, so there's no reason for Jace to be there.

I'm tapping a finger to my chin, racking my brain for inspiration, when a soft voice behind me says, "Well, well. If it isn't the little homewrecker. In the flesh."

I turn, my eyes going wide as I spot Ginger, standing just a few steps above where I'm sitting. "Ho-homewrecker?" I stammer as I come to my feet, my stomach already tying itself in knots.

How on earth could she know that I was on my way to tell Jace how I feel about him? Is she psychic?

I'm about to ask when she offers a more obvious explanation.

"My friend saw you making out with my fiancé in the square a couple of weeks ago," she says, slinking slowly down the steps, fingertips trailing along the wrought iron railing. "She said it was pathetic. How you threw yourself at him even though he kept trying to push you away."

I frown-blink. I don't remember it that way. Not even a little bit.

But I was drunk, I guess, even though I thought I was riding the high of meeting my Kindred Penis.

"But I told her I didn't care," she continues, stopping in front of me, a smile curving her lips. "I'm not threatened by you. Because I know what Jace likes, and it isn't clingy women who look like skinny orphans someone dressed in clothes from the Goodwill. Jace likes curves and confidence and he's in love with me."

"Maybe he is." I ignore the personal attack and suck in another sneeze. Ginger is hurt and we all say unkind things when we're in pain. "But maybe he's not. I just want to talk to him and find out for sure. If he doesn't feel the way I feel, then I'll step aside."

She laughs. "You're kidding me. You honestly think he might be into you? You're deluded, Olivia. Seriously. Even crazier than I thought."

"I'm not crazy," I insist, standing up straighter.

"You got community service for trying to take a bath in the moon," she says, with a hard roll of her eyes. "You're fucking Looney Tunes and everyone in town knows it. Jace only let you kiss him because he felt sorry for you and he's too nice to shove a crazy person on her ass, even if she deserves it."

I clench my jaw, fighting to keep my secret inside of me. Ginger doesn't need to know that Jace and I slept together. It would hurt her, and I don't want to hurt her, even if she's hurting me. I might not have been raised in a small town, but I was raised right. My mother modeled kindness to me every day of her life. It would be disrespectful to her memory to lash out at the woman in front of me.

Even though *she* deserves it…

"I guess we'll just have to agree to disagree then." I nod and take a step back. "Good luck with everything and congratulations on the baby. I'm sure he or she will be a beautiful blessing."

I turn to go, but there's a sharp pinch just above my elbow—Ginger's fingers, digging deep into my skin as she spins me around with enough force to make me stumble.

"Listen to me, you hippie psycho," she whispers, her voice as hate-filled as her aura was that day I saw her coming down these steps. "Stay the fuck away from Jace. You don't talk to him, you don't look at him, you don't even *think* about him or I will make you sorry you ever left the land of fruit and nuts, do you hear me?"

I frown down into her pinched face, forcing myself to take slow, even breaths, refusing to get sucked into her rage energy. Instead, I calmly, evenly ask, "Are you threatening me? Why would you do that? I'm innocent, Ginger."

"You're a home-wrecking slut," she snaps.

"To my knowledge, I haven't done anything with Jace that he didn't want to do. And I care about him. And your baby. I don't want to cause trouble, I truly don't. I just want to make sure no one's making a mistake they're going to regret. You shouldn't marry someone you don't love, Ginger. Not even because there's a baby on the way."

She laughs again, a sharp bark that makes me wince even before she tightens her grip on my elbow. "Good thing Jace and I are crazy in love then, isn't it? We're so in love that we're moving up the wedding."

I frown and squirm my arm, but she holds on tight. "What?"

"We're so in love we can't wait. And Jace couldn't be

happier about it. He's out getting his tux right now, in fact. By this time tomorrow, I will be Mrs. Jace O'Dell and you will still be a crazy bitch with tiny tits." She releases me with a jerk of her hand, making me whimper in spite of myself.

I don't want to give her the satisfaction of knowing she's hurt me, but I can't help it. Her pinching fingers hurt almost as much as the things she said.

Jace is marrying her. Tomorrow. He's out making preparations right now.

It's too late. I'm too late to save him.

And maybe...he doesn't want to be saved. Maybe Ginger's right and I imagined it all—the attraction, the emotion, the certainty that Jace and I are meant to be something so much more than friends.

"We're done here," she says, breezing past me before turning to deliver her parting shot, "Oh, and Jace is sleeping at my place tonight. In my bed. So if you're thinking about going over to his house to throw yourself at him one last time, I'll spare you the drive. And the embarrassment."

She sashays away, hips swiveling with an exaggerated swish-swash that emphasizes her incredible figure. She really is beautiful and sexy. And she'll be even more beautiful when her pregnancy starts to show.

Too bad she's also mean. And nasty.

And not good enough for Jace, not by half. I just wish he knew that the way I do. But he doesn't. He's sleeping at Ginger's place tonight and marrying her tomorrow. We had a chance, a window, but it's closed now, and I have to come to terms with it.

No matter how much it hurts.

I turn to go, to trudge back to my Vespa, sneezes and all. I'm planning to go home and numb my sorrows in another pint of coconut ice cream, a circle of rose quartz, and a rom com while Princess and I snuggle under the covers—she's been scorned in love too, and will empathize with my pain—when something catches my eye.

It's the sign on the door of the doctor's office, the one Ginger was leaving when our paths collided. Turning back, I climb the steps, getting a closer look at the gold lettering that reads—Dr. Newman and Associates, Fertility Specialists.

"Fertility specialists," I murmur aloud, my forehead bunching. Why would she be seeing a fertility specialist? Cassie said that Ginger and Jace got pregnant over two months ago while on a vacation in Mexico. It was an accident or…at least he thinks it was.

An ugly suspicion blooms inside of me.

What if this baby *wasn't* an accident? What if Ginger did this on purpose? Because she knew Jace was an honorable man and would feel obligated to marry the mother of his child?

If it's true, she's the crazy one, using an innocent human life to manipulate the person she claims to love into a choice he isn't ready to make.

I step closer to the door, but even though the lights are on inside, the office is closed and has been for two hours. So what the heck was Ginger doing here after eight in the evening?

I test the door and find it opens into a small room, but the second door into the office is locked. However, there's a gray handle attached to a metal plate set into the wall beneath the receptionist's window. I cross to it, reading the sign above—Specimen Drop Off. With a glance out to the street to make sure no one's watching, I pull the handle, revealing a small drawer, but there's nothing inside it.

But the drawer does have a hole in the bottom…

I lean closer, peering down to see where the hole leads and what Ginger might have dropped off inside. I'm so focused that the knock on the window above takes me completely by surprise.

I jump, yipping as I stand to face the woman smiling at me from the other side of the glass. "Did you forget something?" she asks.

I shake my head, a guilty laugh bubbling from my lips. "Um, no. I mean, yes… I was just…checking. To make sure my girlfriend's drop-off went okay." I fight the urge to wince at the horribly lame excuse, but the pink-cheeked woman doesn't seem to smell the lie stink on me. Thank goodness for the glass.

She simply leans down, plucking two specimen cups from the area beneath the drawer. "I've got two samples and that's all I'm due to test tonight, so it looks like it went just fine."

"Oh, good," I say, backing away with a wave, even though I'm dying to ask what the samples are samples of and what she's testing them for. But the specimen containers are dark blue and she's bound to get suspicious if I start asking intrusive questions. "Well, I'll just be going then."

"Okay." She waves at me. "Results by tomorrow morning." Grinning, she lifts a hand, two fingers twined together. "Fingers crossed."

I cross mine. "Yes. Fingers crossed."

I turn, scurrying down the steps, my thoughts racing.

"What are you up to Ginger?" I mutter, my intuition screaming that something not-right is going on here, something sneaky that Jace deserves to know about before he walks down the aisle.

But what is it?

And can I figure it out before it's too late?

FOURTEEN

Jace

"It's going to be even more perfect! You'll see!" Ginger takes my hand, dragging me toward her front door. "It's all set. All you have to do is show up, baby. Come on inside. It's getting chilly."

We've been sitting on her porch for half an hour, calmly, and then not-so-calmly, discussing her decision to move up the wedding to tomorrow evening.

The wedding that already felt rushed.

The wedding my parents and brothers and friends are already a little pissed off about—seeing as Ginger posted a mass invite on InstaChat before I had the chance to call anyone and personally deliver the news.

The wedding I'm secretly dreading, no matter how many times I've assured myself I'm doing the right thing.

But I guess that's even more reason to get it over with.

Then Ginger and I will be locked in and I can get the hell over myself, buckle down, and start being the kind of husband and father my family deserves. "All right," I say. "But we're going to have to make it up to my mom. She's upset that she didn't get to help plan anything."

"She can plan our reception," she says, twining her fingers through mine as she reaches for the door. "We'll have something lovely at the end of the summer, a party for all our family and friends to help us celebrate and get ready for the baby."

She leans into me, her breasts pressing against my chest. "But in the meantime, I'm ready to start practicing for our honeymoon. I'm dying to be with you again. The pregnancy hormones are making me soooo frisky."

I force a smile as I give her a quick hug and retreat back a step, before she realizes my dick is still on strike. "No, we're going to do it right. Tomorrow. After the wedding, right after I carry you across the threshold."

And after I've scored some Viagra. I've got an appointment with my doctor tomorrow. I never imagined I'd need this kind of help at twenty-five, but desperate times call for desperate measures. And surely Dr. Henson will help me out, considering it's going to be my wedding night.

Wedding night…

Fuck me.

"Good night, see you tomorrow," I say, backing down the steps as Ginger twinkles her fingers flirtatiously.

"Tomorrow, baby. I can't wait. Sleep tight."

BUT I DON'T SLEEP tight, of course.

I barely sleep at all and when I do, I don't dream of my

bride-to-be. I dream of Olivia, naked in the moonlight. Olivia's kiss, Olivia's touch, Olivia whispering that she can't wait to feel me inside her again.

I wake up Friday morning with a raging, Olivia-inspired hard-on and jerk off to memories of the one night I had with her, knowing it will never be enough. I'm going to ache for her for a long, long time.

Maybe the rest of my life.

But when I'm old and gray and looking back at the choices I've made, at least I'll know that I made the right ones. I was a man my kids can be proud to call a father.

Or my kid, singular. At this rate, the chances of me getting Ginger knocked up again aren't looking good.

Scrubbing a hand over my face, I roll out of bed and stumble into the bathroom, avoiding my own haunted gaze in the mirror. I shower, dress, and head to the bar, meeting with Poppy and her older sister, Penelope, who are going to be holding down the fort until Monday morning.

"You're sure you've got everything you need?" I ask, checking the kegs for the third time. "I'm leaving town tonight, right after the ceremony, so speak now or forever hold your peace."

Speak now. Speak now, asshole. Go find Olivia and speak before it's too late. But I ignore my weak-willed inner voice and stay focused on Poppy as she says, "I've got everything under control, boss. And Penelope's never tended bar, but she's catered a gazillion weddings."

"Maybe more." Penelope, a cute woman with big blue eyes and perky blond pigtails, laughs. "We'll keep things running smoothly. Don't worry about a thing, just enjoy your honeymoon."

"It's just a weekend in Atlanta," I say, downplaying it.

Because I don't want to think of it as a honeymoon.

Because I'm in denial about half the shit going on in my life right now.

But so what? Denial is what grown-ups do. They deny themselves permission to do things that are bad for them and force themselves to make reasonable choices.

I eat kale at least twice a week, even though it tastes like stir-fried butt grass. I eat it because it's good for me and keeps my body running smoothly. I can eat Ginger twice a week too, in the name of our child's happiness.

The thought makes my tongue curl in my throat, pulling a dick-like retreat that doesn't bode well. Not well at all.

I leave the bar in the capable hands of the Parker sisters and head off to the doctor's office, where I'm weighed, measured, poked, prodded, and told I'm in excellent health. Perfect health in fact.

"Which makes me think this probably isn't a physical problem." Dr. Henson peeks at me from the corner of her kind brown eyes. She's been my doctor since I was a kid and she's never made me feel bad about my abundance of broken bones or the time I almost lost a thumb because I was too drunk to remember how my buddy's passenger door worked. And I know she isn't trying to lay on a guilt trip now.

Still, I can't bring myself to look her in the eye as I say, "Probably not, but does it matter? It's my wedding night, doc."

"So I saw on InstaChat." She settles down on the rolling stool in front of the exam table. "I also couldn't help but notice you hadn't commented on the post, Jace."

"Been busy," I say with a shrug.

"Too busy to show any excitement about your own wedding?" She leans in, peering up into my downturned face. "It's okay to change your mind, you know. Even about things like this. It might feel like the end of the world, but it won't be. I promise."

I pull in a breath, hold it, counting down from ten until the temptation to spill my guts passes. Then I force a smile and say, "I hope you'll be the baby's doctor too. You do a good job of keeping the O'Dells out of trouble."

She sighs, shaking her head with a smile. "I try anyway." She pats my knee before bustling to her feet, grabbing her clipboard and iPad on her way to the door, where she pauses. "I'll leave the prescription at the front, and I'll see you at the altar. Debbie and I are cutting out early to make it to the church on time."

"Great. Thanks, doc," I say, relieved and freshly stressed at the same time.

I'm going to be able to get it up tonight, but only after standing up in church with Ginger and promising her forever in front of everyone we know.

If only Ginger had been on board with a civil ceremony down at city hall, I don't think I'd be this nervous. But the big public fuss, the chaotic swirl as Ginger and her mother whipped up a big outdoor wedding at the church out of thin air, the tuxedo fitting and the tense conversations with my family and this secret Viagra mission have all combined to make me a hot fucking mess.

I pay my co-pay, collect my script, and pop over to the pharmacy to get it filled, grabbing one of those calming herbal teas Olivia swears by at the bakery while I wait. But the herbs don't calm me. They just remind me of her.

What I need is a drink, dammit. A real drink.

Ass unclenching for the first time today, I pull out my phone and shoot off a text to Blake, the only person I know who might not be at work right now —*Hey baby brother. Up for a quick bachelor party before I get hitched this afternoon?*

I only have to wait a second before he shoots back —*Hell*

yes. Meet you at The Back Door in twenty minutes. I'm buying. We're starting with a shot of whiskey.

Grinning as relief spreads through my chest, I shoot him a *see you there*, grab my pills from the pharmacy, and hit the road, ready to drown my wedding day jitters in alcohol, the way God intended.

FIFTEEN

Olivia

"I wish you were a real detective, Sir Pendleton." I pace back and forth in front of Hope's whiteboard in her office, carefully examining our list of clues.

Sir Pendleton—who I brought to stay with Hope until I can get Princess's humping under control—shoots me a look from the desk that infers that he *is* a real detective and I'm simply not listening hard enough.

"Then talk louder," I mutter. "We're running out of time. The wedding's in two hours."

"Talking to the squirrel again?" Hope asks, breezing in with two cups of turmeric and ginger tea, in hopes the herbs will help clear our heads now that our girls' lunch has turned into a clue gathering session. I told her everything, which is good, because I skipped work today and I've been all over town on my own looking for clues and it turns out I'm not a very good detective.

"Yes. But so far he's refusing to give up the goods." I sneeze, then glare at Sir P. "But he knows something, I can tell. He was there the night it happened."

"The night you fell in love with Jace?" she says, using the L word again.

"The night Jace and I discovered that our auras are naturally complementary. It's not time for the L word, yet," I say, even though it's becoming increasingly clear that what I feel for Jace is so much more than lust.

I don't stay up all night and show up on a new friend's front stoop with a stuffed Inspector at Large and a list of clues for just anyone.

"All right, adding that in." She writes "discovery of Sir Pendleton" next to "discovery and subsequent adoption of Princess von Spooksalot" on the "Things that Could be Relevant" list.

"In the trash," I add. "We found him in the trash."

She scrawls. "Where? Who would throw out such a magnificent specimen?"

"I don't know, but he was in the bins behind the bar. Jace said it was kind of a catch-all place for people to dump unwanted things they're too embarrassed to throw out anywhere else."

"Interesting," she says, lips puckering as she studies the board. "I'll know where to go the next time I need to throw out an old dildo."

I giggle. "Me too. Though I do try to recycle them whenever possible. They make great coat hangers and stands for drying rainboots upside down." I frown. "But if Ginger and Jace get married, I won't be welcome at the Wild Hog anymore. Not even in the back by the trash cans. I swear, I thought she was going to skin me alive last night." I glance down at my elbow, where I'm sporting a set of bruises in the shape of Ginger's fingers and thumb.

"Not going to happen. Let's go over the timeline again," Hope says, taking a sip of tea. "So allegedly, Ginger's friend sees you making out with Jace in the park. She tattles to Ginger, who, miraculously, finds out she's pregnant a few days later and Jace calls you, saying he's sorry but that his ex is knocked up and he has to do the right thing and stand by his baby mama."

I bob my head from side to side. "More or less. Yes."

"Blast ahead to last week, when you see Ginger coming out of a fertility doctor's office, and this week to her dropping off a mysterious sample after hours at the same office. Where, even though she claims that she isn't at all concerned that you're a threat to her relationship, she still tried to pinch your arm off."

"Yes. But according to Jace, they got pregnant in Mexico a good month and a half before he and I…"

"Bumped auras?" She smirks and I blush, but not because I'm shy about my sexuality. I just don't want to share too much about that night. With anyone, even a friend. It's special, private, something I want to remember with Jace and no one else.

I nod. "Yes. So why is she seeing a fertility specialist? The only thing that makes sense is that she was trying to get pregnant before they left for Mexico and now she's under a specialist's care for the high-risk pregnancy. Which would mean she did this on purpose, without asking Jace's permission. Which is a violation."

"Agreed, a total violation," she says, smile falling away. "But if that's what happened, it doesn't explain her timing with the big reveal."

I chew my lip as a posh British voice in my head says, *Timing is everything, dear Olivia.*

I cut a sharp glance Sir Pendleton's way and for a moment I would swear I see his moustache wiggle.

"Timing *is* everything, I agree," I say, pacing to one end of the office and back to the other. "So the options are A, she didn't know she was pregnant yet and the timing was just a coincidence."

Hope wrinkles her nose. "Could be. Convenient, but maybe."

"B, she knew she was pregnant, but was waiting to tell Jace for some reason. Maybe because the pregnancy is high-risk. She might have wanted to wait until the three-month mark, but was pushed into fessing up earlier when she thought she might be losing him."

"I think we're getting warmer," she says, pointing a finger at my chest.

"Or…" I slow to a stop as that posh voice echoes again between my ears, warning me that *The simplest answer is almost always the correct answer.*

And what is the simplest answer? Not that Ginger has been secretly undergoing fertility treatments for months as part of a covert scheme to get Jace to marry her that only rolled into motion once he and I were caught making out in the park. No, the simplest answer is, "She's faking it," I blurt out, pulse picking up as the pieces click into place. "She's faking the pregnancy. There is no baby."

Hope's eyes go wide. "No way. She wouldn't."

I pace again, tapping my chin with my finger as I go. "Maybe she realized that Jace was slipping away so she lied about being pregnant in order to get him back. And now she's scrambling, trying to get pregnant by any means necessary before Jace learns the truth."

"Which means that sample last night was…" She arches a brow.

I shake my head. "I don't know. Maybe…sperm? Jace's sperm? Taken without his knowledge somehow?" But even as the words leave my mouth they feel wrong.

"That would be messed up. And kind of hard to manage, don't you think? I mean...don't guys usually know if their boys are being collected? How else would she get it in the specimen cup?"

I wave a hand in the air, inspiration striking as another sneeze fit attacks me. "Wait a minute, wait a minute. There's something we've missed. Ginger's friend, who was there that night, watching us. She had to be the person who dumped Princess in the park! There was no one else around, just the cage, Jace and me, and the moonlight." I wiggle my fingers. "And Sir Pendleton and Princess, but the point is—Ginger's friend is a hedgehog abandoner!"

Hope gives me a long blank look. "Really? That's the thing we've missed in our hunt for the truth about Ginger's baby and her weird behavior?"

I bite my thumb. "Okay, that's probably not the most important thing, but it's upsetting. And it proves Ginger has bad friends. What kind of monster abandons a sweet little hedgehog in the park, where she could get eaten by wild dogs? Especially when there's a perfectly amazing pet shelter right here in town. I mean, look at the number of cats you've taken in this month alone. You clearly won't turn any deserving creature away."

"Oh my God..." She leaps to her feet, sloshing tea over the edge of her cup. "The cats!"

I freeze, going motionless for fear of disrupting her breakthrough. "Yes? The cats?"

She bounces up and down. "The cats! Ginger was helping me clean all the litter boxes! And you're not supposed to do that when you're pregnant because of a risk of toxoplasmosis. I didn't think about it at the time—though I should have, bad Hope—but that's a pregnancy no-no."

I clap my hands. "There! Real evidence that she's faking." I sag, my sudden elation fleeing as quickly as it arrived. "But not really. She just might not have known. I mean, she's never had a baby before."

"She's going to a fertility doctor and she doesn't know all the preggo rules? Doubtful."

"Doubtful, but possible." I exhale sharply, feeling every second ticking by like a sharp little claw scratching away at my sanity. I have to find proof that Ginger is lying and therefore unworthy of Jace before she walks down the aisle, because even *I* know that running over to stop the wedding just because their auras are incompatible won't work. Not in this town. "We need something else. Something real."

"Something like sperm." Hope stands, plunking her mug down beside Sir Pendleton. "Get your purse. We're going to that fertility clinic."

I hesitate. "But we can't. I mean, we can, but they won't tell us anything. They can't. Doctor-patient confidentiality."

"So we'll become patients." Her brown eyes narrow deviously, making her resemble a non-squirrel Sir Pendleton as she swirls an imaginary moustache. "Or at least make them *think* we're becoming patients until we get the dirt on the drop-offs. What they're dropping and why... If it's sperm, we'll know Ginger is up to something bad, and you'll have enough evidence to stop the wedding."

"Not evidence. It will still be conjecture." I meet her scheming gaze with one of my own. "Unless I steal the sperm sample, hustle it over to the church, and present it to Jace as a 'Don't Get Married' present..."

She whoops. "Now you're talking! Let's go, woman. We have sperm to steal and a wedding to stop."

SIXTEEN

Olivia

By the time Hope and I are finally shown into Dr. Newman's office in the fertility clinic, we only have forty minutes left before the ceremony starts. It's all I can do not to grab him by the shoulders and beg him to give up the goods on the specimen cups, but I force myself to follow him quietly down the hall to his office.

He steps inside, glancing between Hope and me as he makes his way to his desk. "So you two would like to have a baby?" he asks, peering at us over his spectacles.

"Yes," we both answer, because this is the plan we worked out in the waiting room when the receptionist insisted that the doctor would have to be the one to answer our questions.

"I was…unaware that you were together," he says.

"With all the fuss everyone made over Bill at the feed store and his dresses, we decided to keep it on the down-low," Hope says quickly while I remind myself that sometimes little lies are necessary for the sake of big love.

And also while I sneeze. Again.

He nods. "That's understandable."

"I've also been meaning to get in here to ask you about a fertility issue I'm having with my alpaca," she adds. "Actually, with my specimen storage refrigerator. It keeps going on the fritz, and I was wondering if I could rent some storage space from you since I can't seem to get mine to work right."

"She's a Wiper," I say helpfully. "It's not her fault. But Chewpaca is a beautiful alpaca stud who deserves to have all the baby alpacas and make a huge beautiful family."

"That's a question for my office manager," Dr. Newman tells us. "Which of you will be carrying the human baby?"

"Is it okay if we haven't picked a sperm donor yet?" I ask instead of answering, because the clock is ticking. My nose twitches, but I hold in my next sneeze. I don't have time for a sneezing fit. I have a wedding to stop. "And can we just have him drop off the sample in your little drawer outside? Or do you have pre-made samples we can choose from?"

His watery blue eyes are bulging behind his glasses.

This isn't good. I should've brought Sir Pendleton to ask the questions for us.

"She's never done this before," Hope tells him while she pats me on the back. "Or helped me with Chewpaca."

"We don't—" He clears his throat and pulls off his glasses to wipe them on his lab coat while he continues. "We require all sperm donations to be made in person. In the office."

"Then what's your little drawer thingie for?"

His brows slant together. "Urine samples, Ms. Moonbeam."

Hope and I gape at each other. *Urine samples*? What will *urine samples* prove?

That Ginger's not pregnant, my dear Ms. Moonbeam that proper British voice in my head suggests.

"Lab results!" I exclaim.

"Yes, Ms. Moonbeam. We test the samples in our lab," the doctor says.

Making eye contact with Hope, I jerk my head toward the door. One of us needs to get Ginger's lab results!

"Could I see your storage facility?" she blurts. "No, wait. I want to check it out, but I don't want to *short* it out. Can Olivia maybe see your storage facility?"

He slides his glasses back on and narrows his eyes at both of us as I let a little sneeze through. "Are you ladies actually involved and interested in medical treatment to get pregnant, or is this all about an alpaca?"

Hope and I trade glances again.

And then she bursts into tears. "It's Chewpaca," she wails. "I'm so, so worried that I've ruined all his sperm and he's the best alpaca with so much stud potential. But my cryogenic fridge keeps going on the fritz and it's such an ordeal to get the samples from him—you understand, of course—and now we have to start all over. His lineage is beyond reproach but he was denied female companionship for so long that he—he—he's masturbating all the good sperm away and unable to perform with the ladies. It's really a tragic loss to the alpaca community and the world at large." She reaches a hand out, resting it on his desk, creating a nearly-invisible ripple in the air. But I see it, and the doctor certainly feels it.

He suddenly jerks straight, his attention shifting to his now-crackling computer. He taps the keyboard, then hits the button on the monitor.

He hits it again. And again. But the spark has left the building.

"Oh, no, and now I've ruined your computer," Hope adds with a truly contrite moan. "I did, didn't I? I killed your monitor. Oh my god, I am *so sorry*."

"Dr. Newman?" someone calls outside the office. "Is everything okay?"

Rising from his desk, he flings the door open and gestures her inside. "My screen just went black. Totally black."

"What? Let me see."

"Olivia," Hope whimpers, swiping at her cheeks. "Can you—get me—tissues?"

She slides me a meaningful look, one that isn't teary-eyed at all, like she really is doing this all on command. I make a mental note to ask her about her acting background later, but not now. I leap to my feet. "Yes! Of course! Tissues!"

I dart out the door, keeping an eye out for more nurses as I slink toward... Well, I don't actually know *what* I'm slinking toward.

I need to find the lab.

Or the patient file room.

Yes! The patient file room. Or a computer.

Except can I really do that? People's medical information is private. It's personal. If Ginger tricked Jace into getting her pregnant, that was a violation of his trust, but it would also be a violation of human decency—and the law—to snoop in her medical records.

Gah.

But I have to prove she's not pregnant so Jace won't marry her!

How else can I prove it without her medical records?

I freeze when I hear a voice on the other side of the

nearest door. "I'm so sorry, Ms. Smith. I wish I had better news, but we can try again next month. Yes, yes, of course. We'll get you on the schedule. How does…"

I gasp and slink back against the door.

Ginger's not pregnant.

I *knew* it!

"Ma'am? Can I help you?"

The nurse who went into Dr. Newman's office is in the hallway frowning at me.

"Tissues!" I exclaim. I sneeze again. "I need tissues."

"There are tissues on Dr. Newman's desk."

"Oh. Right. I knew that. I was just so—Hope was so upset—I was overcome—"

"You and Ms. St. Claire should probably come back another day." Her tone implies *or not at all*, because we're possibly the worst potential patients in the history of patients, but *Ginger's not pregnant.*

"Um, okay," I agree. I need to go. I have a wedding to stop.

Hope steps out of the doctor's office, still sniffling but very much improved. "Yes, of course we'll schedule a regular appointment next time," she says. "And I really would love your advice on Chewpaca."

"Thank you." I link my arm with hers, pulling her toward the front door. "Thank you *so much.*"

As soon as we're outside, I whisper, "Ginger's not pregnant! I heard a nurse on the phone *telling* her so. Well, I mean, she said *Ms. Smith*, but that has to be Ginger, right? How many Smiths can there be in Happy Cat?"

Her face falls. "At least seven off the top of my head, and five of them are women of childbearing age."

"But—but—"

"I'm not saying you're wrong," she tells me. "But it's not conclusive. And it's not like we can force her to pee on a stick in public to prove to us that she *is* pregnant. You didn't get into the lab or file room or whatever?"

I'm wringing my hands, because I'm a total and complete failure. "It just seemed like such a personal violation," I whisper.

"Aw, Olivia." She pulls me into a hug. "You are *such* a good person. And that's why you have to go stop this wedding. *Now*. I think you're the only person who can do it. C'mon. I'll drive you over."

We pop over to her truck and she cranks the engine. We only have thirty minutes to get to the wedding, but we're going to make it.

We are.

It's at the little church past the rescue farm, so she points the truck toward home. "C'mon, c'mon, c'mon," she says as we putter out of downtown Happy Cat, past the factory, and through the neighborhoods that lead to the farm just beyond the edge of town.

But her truck is slowing down.

"What's happening?" I ask.

"No, no, *no*," she groans.

The truck shakes and shivers. I gasp and put a hand to the dashboard.

"Fucking electricity," she sighs as something pops and the truck sputters to a halt half a mile from the farm. She cranks the engine, but it won't turn over, and the wedding's in twenty-five minutes and *I have to stop it*.

She leaps out. "You try!" she says. "See if you can get it started without me inside to screw things up and take my truck! I'll catch up!"

I slide into the driver's seat and turn the key, but something whines and clicks beneath the steering wheel and the engine in the ancient truck refuses to turn over. "It won't start!" I call to her. "*It won't start!*"

"Your scooter!" she hollers. "Go get your Vespa!"

I leap out of the truck and take off at a mad dash down the road, occasionally sneezing, flip-flops slapping the concrete and crocheted mini-dress flapping around my legs, revealing more thigh than appropriate for the side of a public highway—even a rural one—but I have to do this.

I absolutely *must* stop the wedding. Jace deserves better. He doesn't love Ginger. Not enough to marry her. And she's *lying*. She's lying and tricking him and it doesn't matter that I don't have proof, because I *know* she's lying. I *know* she's not pregnant.

"Keep looking for proof!" I call over my shoulder to Hope as I dash up the road.

"Will do," she shouts. "Good luck!"

Yes. Good luck. I need all of it I can get.

I have to make it.

I have to make it in time.

A man's entire future depends on it.

SEVENTEEN

From the texts of the O'Dell brothers

Blake: Clint, man, you'd better be awake, because we need a tie-breaker. Now.

Clint: For what?

Blake: Should Jace marry Ginger tonight, yes or no?

Clint: WTF? TONIGHT? No. Definitely not.

Ryan: WRONG. He needs to step up and do the right thing.

Blake: The "right thing" is taking care of the baby, not dooming himself to a toxic, loveless marriage.

Jace: *pickle emoji* *pickle emoji* *laughing emoji* *hangman emoji*

Clint: Why is Jace using emojis? He hates emojis.

Blake: He's drunk off his ass at The Back Door. Ryan's trying to make him go get married. I'm trying to keep him here.

Jace: Pickle Dick. HAHAHAHA. My pickle dick is broke. *pickle emoji*

Clint: He can't get married shit-faced.

Ryan: I'm not saying I'm a big fan of Ginger, but he needs to get some legal protection. He told us she threatened to run away and never let him see the baby. He HAS to marry her, drunk or not.

Blake: Bullshit. This is what the cops are for.

Ryan: In this town? With Chester Assface on his case?

Clint: Are you dumbasses seriously sitting in a bar and texting me instead of talking to each other?

Jace: *handcuff emoji* *dragon emoji* *heart emoji* *rainbow emoji*

Blake: Well, yeah. I mean, we get emojis out of Loverboy here this way.

Ryan: I'm done discussing this. Jace has to get married. End of story. I don't fucking like it, but it's the only option.

Jace: *cheese emoji* *fart emoji* *sneeze emoji* HAHA-

HAHA my life ducks. Ducks. DUCKS! Why won't it let me write DUCKS?!

Blake: He can't get married like this.

Clint: Jace. Dude. If you're that drunk, you can't get married.

Jace: *olive emoji* *eggplant emoji* *squirrel emoji* *sneeze emoji*

Ryan: I agree it would be more ideal if this wasn't so rushed, but we don't have time to discuss it. We have to get to the ceremony NOW.

Blake: C'mon, Clint. Tell him he's wrong.

Clint: Fuck. I don't like it, but he's not wrong. Jace needs some legal claim to the kid if she's threatening to run away.

Ryan: See? Two on one. We're out of here.

Blake: Are you fucking kidding me? Stick up for love, man. What would you do if some guy were forcing Cassie to marry him because he was knocked up?

Ryan: Well there's the fact that MEN CAN'T CARRY BABIES. So WTF kind of argument is that?

Blake: Christ. You're as bad as Hope.

Clint: Dude. Wait your turn. We need to get Jace married off first.

Blake: WTF?

Ryan: Heh. Nice one. You want us to dial you in on a video call to watch the ceremony?

Clint: Hell, no. I said he needs to get married. I didn't say I wanted to watch it.

Jace: ASSHOLES. O can smell tree!

Blake: That was "I can still read," Clint. Since he can't TYPE.

Clint: Jace, you want to get married? You're the one with a vote here.

Ryan: He's thinking.

Blake: If he has to think, he shouldn't do it. Marriage is about love and commitment and knowing you're doing the right thing without a shade of fucking doubt.

Clint: Thank you, Professor Blake, for that DUH moment. Jace, bud, you need a phone call?

Jace: *ring emoji* *champagne emoji* *bride emoji* *olive emoji*

Blake: You want a martini with your getaway car?

Ryan: SHUT UP. He's getting married, and we're ALL going to be there to help him through whatever comes next. Got it?

Blake: Sometimes I regret that you have so much blackmail material on me.

Ryan: FUCK. Ceremony's in seven minutes. We're out of here. Clint, call me if you want to watch.

Clint: Can I watch later? After I'm drunk? It's still morning here.

Three minutes later...

Clint: Hello? You assholes still there?

Two minutes later...

Clint: Fuck…. Good luck, Jace.

EIGHTEEN

Jace

Getting married isn't so bad. I have the hiccups, so that's fun.

I grin.

Olivia had the hiccups, the night I fell in love with her.

I really love Olivia. I'm so glad we're getting married...

Ginger's face swims into view at the back of the carpet someone rolled out on the grass outside the church — reminding me I'm not marrying Olivia — and my smile goes as limp as my pickle dick.

I miss having a cucumber dick. A big cucumber. Fresh. Hardy. Confident.

The kind that could win a blue ribbon at the fair.

I want a blue ribbon cucumber dick again. Good dick. Win that prize.

That prize in the sky.

I tilt my head back, staring up. Ah, that blue blue sky. As pretty as Olivia's eyes.

If I have to go to my own funeral, at least I'm going while the sun is shining, before the storm I can feel blowing in hits. My nose knows a summer storm, even when my nose is drunk.

And my nose is wasted, nearly as trashed as my brain.

Tomorrow is *not* going to be pretty.

But it's pretty right now! Pretty outside. Pretty arch thingie with flowers over my head. Pretty preacher dude. Nice shiny bald head. He's going to officiate the hell out of this funeral.

Wedding.

Not funeral.

How many shots did I have?

I need one more. Definitely one more.

My mom's crying in the front row, I can hear her, even though she's trying to keep it quiet.

Funeral?

No. Wedding. I'm getting hitched.

While I'm hammered.

Ginger wants me to hammer her too, which is going to be a problem since I'm pretty sure I left the Viagra at the bar.

"You gonna make it, buddy?" a soft voice asks.

Whoa. Ryan's next to me. Aw, Ryan. I love that fucker. He's like a second dad to me, to all of us, really. Always knows what I'm supposed to do. He helped me open my bar. Co-signed the fleece.

I snicker to myself.

Lease. Not *fleece*.

"Jace?" Ryan mutters.

Ginger's floating down the carpet between the seats set

up on the grass on an army of little flower men. She has three feet. That's weird.

One must be for the baby.

God…the baby.

"Shid, gonna be a dad," I tell Ryan.

The pretty preacher guy's wrinkled face wrinkles more. "Mr. O'Dell, are you in your cups?"

"Nopes," I tell him. "No cups. None."

"Nerves," Ryan says. "And he always stinks like this when he sweats."

Blake coughs something from behind Ryan. Like *bullshit*.

Good thing we're outside the church. Or he'd be struck by lightning for that. Or maybe *I'd* be struck by lightning for marrying the wrong girl.

Cause that's definitely Ginger, not my Liv. Ginger, in a white fluffy dress with big cleavage. *Big* cleavage. All three of her cleavages.

The army of flower petals stops next to me, and she smiles a huge smile that makes my gut roll over like someone slapped it with a dead fish.

I feel like singing, a country song I compose in my head that goes, *I used to love her, but she loved to flirt, and all the time I loved her, she treated me like dirt. Now I'm in love with Olivia, but Ginger's having my baby, and so I'm gonna marry her, because it's what I say-bied.*

"Dearly befuddled," the preacher says, and I chortle, because that's not the line.

Fuck, is my hair sweating?

I think my hair's sweating.

My hair's sweating, and my ears are broken. Or missing.

What if I left my ears at the bar too? The wedding pictures are going to look fucking weird, that's what.

Ginger takes my hand. "I'm so happy, Jacey. We're going to be *so good* together," she whispers.

I'm really glad this is just a bad dream.

Except she feels super real. And there's a mosquito on my hand that just bit me, and that hurt. I slap it away, and Ginger frowns.

My mom sobs harder.

"Jaaaaaacccccceeeeee!" someone calls. "Sstttt-toooooooopppppp!"

The call ends on a series of sneezes.

Is that…

I turn, squinting toward the church.

Blond hair is flowing behind a gorgeous woman on a motorbike with a sidecar.

"What the *hell*?" Ginger hisses, and suddenly I'm not feeling so drunk anymore.

No, if I was drunk, I couldn't feel that cold slither of dread wrapping around my chest and crawling all over my skin, starting right where Ginger's latched onto my wrist.

"Don't do it!" Olivia yells. "You can't!"

"Jacey, you're not going to let her ruin our wedding day, are you?" Ginger whispers, her eyes wide and terrified, except…not.

They're more…calculated.

Like she wants me to *think* she's terrified of having our wedding day ruined.

Our wedding day.

Wedding.

Marriage.

I can't get married.

I seriously can't get married. It will kill me. Maybe not right away, but eventually, bit by bit, all those daily betrayals mounting up until my life is nothing but a lie.

But I don't want to lie. I want to tell the truth and the

truth is Olivia. Olivia, who's bouncing her Vespa from the church down the grass toward us, occasionally sneezing. People are gasping and shrieking.

Ryan puts a hand to my shoulder. "What the—" he starts, but Olivia spins her Vespa between me and my parents in the front row and stops it short with the sidecar between us.

She looks at me, then at Ginger, *real* terror clouding her pretty eyes. When she looks at me again, she doesn't pause.

"You can't marry her!" She reaches over and yanks on my arm, and I fall.

I tumble into the sidecar, and then it's moving, tearing up the aisle that Ginger just floated down. Taking me away.

Rescuing me.

There'll be hell to pay for this later.

But right now, I'm not going anywhere. I'm going to hunker down and hang on for the ride.

NINETEEN

Olivia

I stole a groom.

I shoplifted a husband.

I absconded with a man so drunk that he passes out before we reach the city limits, snoring so loudly I can hear him over the rumble of the tires on gravel as I turn off the highway and head east on the first of many dirt roads leading to the other side of town.

I have to stay off the main throughways, just in case. There's a chance someone at the wedding may have called the sheriff, even though it was clear Jace willingly took that tumble into my sidecar.

At least I think he did…

"You were willing, right?" I wait, but he's still out cold as I cut through one corner of the MacIntoshes's pasture to hook up with the bike trail leading through the woods not far from Savannah's place. But instead of turning left toward civilization, I turn right, pushing deeper into the woods on a narrow trail barely big enough for a car.

I can't take Jace anywhere Ginger might think to look for us. Not until I get him sobered up and lay out all my evidence. Or my suspicions. Strong suspicions.

Good gravy, I've abducted a man from his wedding based on *strong suspicions*. I'm clearly as out of my mind as Ginger thinks I am, but I don't regret it. I did what I had to do, and I'm prepared to face the consequences.

Even if that means he ends up hating me for ruining his wedding.

But hopefully he'll see that I was only trying to help. To show my love for him, even if it was an...unconventional display.

I'm in love with him. I really am. As I park outside my secret she shed deep in the wilderness and turn to stare down at Jace's sleeping face, there's no more denying it. I'm *so* happy to be with him again. Even when he's passed out and smells like a distillery, he's still got the world's best vibes.

But they're going to be very damp vibes if I don't get him inside soon. In the past half hour the wind has picked up, sending rain clouds swooping in. Thunder rumbles in the distance, lifting the hairs on the back of my neck as I grab him under the arms and pull, succeeding in lifting him less than an inch out of the sidecar before he slumps back down again.

"Think, Olivia," I mutter, scanning the ground outside the cozy makeshift cottage. It was probably a hunting camp originally. When I stumbled across it, it had clearly been abandoned. Now, it's painted with butterflies and flowers on the outside, surrounded by the woods like a magical fairy cabin, with wildflowers growing beneath the canopy of oaks and maples. I added yard gnomes to dance with the squirrels and chipmunks. One day, if the original owner ever comes back, I'll surrender my hiding spot. But for now, it's my little bit of magic to share with the woodland creatures—on the outside, anyway—complete with a fire pit surrounded by thick fallen logs that serve as benches, my secret getaway when the world gets hard.

The spaces between the benches are stacked with wood for the fire pit, but they're short logs, nothing big enough to use as a lever to pry Jace out of my Vespa.

Note to self: The next time you steal a groom, bring a lever.

Or a forklift.

Considering he has at least six inches and fifty pounds on me, something more sophisticated than a simple machine might be required.

"Fuuuuuuuu," he groans, sucking in a breath and pressing a hand to his forehead before continuing with still-closed eyes, "uuuuuuuuuck me."

Awake! He's awake.

"How are you feeling?" I crouch down beside the side-car, bringing my face level with his, crossing my fingers that he's not going to wake up and demand I take him back to the church.

He hums, low and rough, and straightens himself in the sidecar with a wince. "Not so good. I think I got run over by a rhinoceros."

"Nope, you just got really drunk, I think."

"Am I married?"

"No," I whisper.

"Am I dreaming?"

"No."

"What year is it?"

"The same year it was an hour ago. When I kidnapped you. From your wedding," I say with a nervous laugh. "So hopefully you don't want to run *me* over with a rhinoceros. I didn't realize you were drunk until after the whole dragging you into my scooter part."

His dark green eyes slit open, connecting with mine with an intensity that makes my breath catch. "I would never run you over. With anything." He reaches out, covering my hand with his, pressing it tighter to the warm metal on the edge of the sidecar. "Thank you. I'm pretty sure you just saved my fucking life."

"Oh, good," I whisper, pulse racing so fast it's hard to form words, hard to think of anything but how grateful I am to be here with him, to be looking into his eyes and seeing nothing but gratitude and relief, to know I did the right thing, and he thinks so too. "I had a good reason."

"I hope it's because you like me," he murmurs, his face moving closer to mine. "Because I like the hell out of you. Even halfway between drunk and hungover, you make me happy to be alive."

"Me too. So happy." My heart is soaring. I know I need to tell him *why* I kidnapped him, but it can wait. *Why* doesn't seem to matter. Not when us being here, together, our auras crackling happily around us, feels so very right.

For the first time in weeks, I'm right where I'm supposed to be.

"Thank you," he says in that low, semi-intoxicated gravel. His thick hair is disheveled and his eyes bloodshot, but not as bad as they were. "Thank you for being you. Perfect, adorable, understanding, saving-my-life you."

And then he kisses me and I'm instantly even happier. Fireworks shoot across the sky and delight shivers through me, every fiber of my body and soul celebrating being close to him again.

"You taste like whiskey," I murmur against his lips.

"And you taste like heaven. Like the sweetest thing I've

ever tasted. Except maybe one other thing..." He drags me into the sidecar, sending me tumbling across his lap, but my bleat of surprise is barely out of my mouth before it becomes a moan of pleasure.

Because his hand is sliding up my thigh. "I want you, Liv. I want you so bad."

"*Yes*," I gasp. "Oh, Jace — I want you too."

His fingers drift under my skirt and push aside my panties and then he's touching me there — *there*, where I'm already hot and wet from a single, whiskey-flavored kiss.

"I want my mouth right here." Jace kisses me harder as his fingers tease between my legs, rubbing my clit in slow, sultry circles before pushing inside me, making me gasp. "I can't wait to hear the sounds you make when you come, Liv. God, I'm so ducking hard. I mean fucking," he says, huffing softly against my neck. "Fucking hard. God, it feels so good to be hard for you with you actually close enough to touch."

"You're drunk." I shiver as he urges my legs wider apart and pushes deeper, until his fingers are hitting a delicious place inside me while the heel of his palm rubs against an even sweeter spot. "We shouldn't... We... Oh god, we..."

"Yes. *We*." His teeth rake lightly over my neck, making my pulse spike. "I want to be we, Liv. And I want you coming for me. I'm not too drunk to make you feel good. I've wanted to make you feel good for weeks. Months. Longer."

Threading my fingers into his hair, I stop fighting the pressure building between my hips. I hold on to him with my hands and let go with my heart, my head falling back with a cry as the fireworks explode again, followed by a loud boom.

Not fireworks. Lightning and thunder. Close.

The thought — and the last shudders of my orgasm —

have barely danced into my conscious mind when fat rain-drops begin to fall, plunking down on us as we kiss. "Inside," I say, flinching as the drops fall harder. "We should get inside."

"Is there a bed inside?"

I nod. "Yes, but we should talk. And you're drunk and —whoa!" My words end in a whoop as Jace scoops me up and rolls out of the sidecar with me still in his arms. He stumbles as he tries to find his footing, but he doesn't drop me, and a moment later he's sprinting for the front of the shed like he's running away from a pack of wild dogs, not a little thunder and lightning.

But he isn't running *away* from anything at all. He's running *toward*.

Toward the door and the bed.

And me.

"We really should wait until you're sober," I insist as he kicks the door to my forest lady lair closed behind us and lays me down on the quilt-covered bed against the wall in the small room. "You know I don't like to take advantage."

"Stop." He stretches out beside me, pressing a finger to my lips. "You could never take advantage of me. First, because you're too damned sweet to take advantage of anyone. And second, because all I want to do—whether I'm sober, wasted, or somewhere in between—is make love to you."

Euphoria pulses through my aura as he rolls me under him with a smile nearly as wide as the one making my jaw ache. "Really?"

"Really," he assures me, nudging my legs apart and settling between them, making my lashes flutter as I feel how thick and hard he is behind the fly of his tuxedo pants. "And we're going to be together when we're both sober, I promise. I'm going to get to that as soon as fucking possible." He kisses me slow, deep, and delicious before he whispers, "But in the meantime I'm dying to show you what you do to me, Liv. All the things you make me feel."

"You make me feel all the things too," I say, shocked to sense tears pressing at the backs of my eyes. "I like you so much, Jace."

"Me too. More than like you." He pauses, pulling back to gaze down into my face for a long, fizzy moment that makes me feel even more things. Because he's looking straight through my aura, into my heart, my soul, and he's not looking away. Not for a second. "I know this is going to sound crazy, especially considering I was about to marry another woman before you saved me, but...I love you, Liv."

"R-really?" I stammer, my throat squeezing tight with a mixture of wonder and gratitude.

"Really," he promises, still meeting my gaze. No flinching. "I love your sweetness and your silliness and the way you're always looking out for other people."

I blink faster, so overwhelmed I can't get "I love you too" out before he pushes on.

"I love that you're not afraid to be yourself—all the time, even when it's hard. Even when you're alone, on the outside looking in, because people don't have the sense to realize what a magical person you are." He cups my face in his palms and I fight to hold back tears.

I don't want to cry. I want to tell Jace all the things I treasure about him too, but I didn't expect this. I'm completely unprepared. I mean, I knew we were compatible and that our auras hummed together in perfect harmony.

I didn't realize that he *saw* me, *truly* saw me, like this.

Not many people ever have. My mother, Savannah and Cassie, and maybe now, Hope, but...that's about it. Most people tend to take in the blond hair, colorful clothes, and purse full of crystals and see me as a character if they're kind, a joke, if they're not.

But not Jace, not this man whose eyes are as familiar as looking in the mirror. I feel like I've known him my entire life.

Or maybe that's just how long I've been waiting for him.

"But I get it," he says in a tender voice that goes straight to my heart. "From the second you walked into the Hog with Savannah, bringing the sun in with you, and talking to every old coot at my bar like he was a good man who deserved the time and attention of a beautiful woman like you, I was a goner. You are the sun, Liv. And if you give me the chance, I'll keep the promise I made the night we found Princess. Or the promise I should have made." He traces my eyebrow with a reverence that makes me feel like a priceless work of art. "I'll never stop being thankful that you're in my life or grateful that I was lucky enough to find you. And I'll never take you for granted. I'll make you feel like the most adored woman on the planet or die trying."

I shake my head fast, back and forth. "No. No dying. That isn't allowed. You have to stay with me and kiss me and laugh with me and love me for a very long time before that happens. And I'm going to do the same." I pause, a little shy now that the words are on the tip of my tongue. But there's no reason to be shy. Because Jace feels the way I feel. Even if he hadn't just said all those beautiful things, it's written all over his face. "Because I love you too."

"Yeah?" His eyes are shining and I just know this is a first for him.

Just like it's a first for me when I wrap my legs tight around his waist and confess, "Yes. I'm completely crazy about you. You make my aura light up like the Fourth of July and I'm pretty sure I've never been this frisky. Ever. In my entire life."

"Only pretty sure?" He rocks against me, rubbing his delicious hard-on against me through our clothes, making my body sing. "So what's it going to take? To make you completely sure?"

"That's a good start." I loop my arms around his neck with a sigh. "Very good."

"Oh, sweetheart, I haven't even gotten started. Just you wait. I'm going to make you forget any man has ever touched you. Any man but me." He kisses me, long and hard, making my breath come fast and my heart sing.

I'm in love with Jace. He's in love with me!

And as he reaches for the bottom of my dress and whips it over my head, I know that this is just our beginning.

TWENTY

Jace

My life has been such a whirlwind the last several weeks, but being saved from my wedding as a thunderstorm rolls in feels like the least crazy part of all of it. Now, I'm shucking my pants and tossing my phone to the floor next to the bed. My brain is still foggy, but my heart is finally clear.

Turns out confession is as good for sobering a man up as it is for his soul. Maybe I wasn't as drunk as I was panicked. And now, I'm so thankful. I don't want to forget a second of this, of making love to the most amazing woman on the planet.

I know there will be consequences to loving Olivia, and that I need to check in with my family, to tell them I'm okay, but climbing back onto the bed with her is so fucking right. "I've been dreaming about you every night," I tell her.

"I've been trying so hard to do the right thing, but

what's right and what's *right* felt so different," she whispers, and I get it.

I completely get it.

"*This* is right." I trace the constellation on her chest with my fingers, then follow my fingers with my tongue. "Olivia, I want you so bad."

"Are you sure? Really sure?"

"Every minute, every hour, every day," I assure her.

When she doesn't answer right away, I lift my head. Her beautiful gemstone eyes search mine, and a wide smile crosses her features, and I swear I'm going to spend every day the rest of my life coaxing that smile out of her.

Making her happy.

Being the man she needs me to be.

"I love your smile," I whisper. "It lights up my entire world."

Thunder booms outside, and she wiggles her hips under me while she strokes her hands down my chest. "Your smile is a gift."

"Your lips are a gift."

"Kiss me?"

"And so much more," I promise.

I'm going to do this right. Make her feel so good, inside and out. Not just her body, but her spirit and her aura and her energetic body and everything else she believes in, because she makes me believe in *me*. In *us*.

She makes me feel worthy.

And I want to prove I am.

I start with her lips, caressing them with mine, kissing her slow and deep and long, stroking her soft skin, exploring her curves, her peaks and valleys, learning where she likes to be stroked harder, softer, where she's ticklish, and what makes her moan, and soon I've got her out of her dress, her gorgeous breasts bare to my mouth as I lick and suck and tease, making her squirm and gasp my name as the storm picks up and rain pelts the thirsty ground outside.

"Oh, please," she begs, her fingers tangling in my hair. "Please, Jace. Now. I don't want to wait. I feel like I've been waiting forever for you."

"My entire life," I say, because it's true. I've been waiting my entire life for being naked with a woman, being *intimate* with a woman, to feel this natural, this perfect and shameless. "But what about protection?"

"There are condoms in the headboard," she says, blushing as she points over her head in the fading light. "I almost brought my boyfriend here last fall, before he turned out to be a jerk face."

"Good," I say, not the least bit concerned about who might have been in her bed before me. Because I'm going to pull out every trick in my erotic arsenal to make sure I'm the last. "I want to keep you safe."

"I always feel safe with you," she breathes, shuddering when I brush my thumb across the tight tip of her nipple. "Safe and...hungry."

"Starving," I echo, devouring her lips again, making her breathless before I kiss my way south, lingering at her perfect shell of a belly button as I strip her panties down her thighs. "And dying for more of this sweetness." I slide two fingers into her heat, coating them with slickness before bringing them to my mouth.

I lift my gaze, watching her watch me as I suck the taste of her from my own skin, cock straining the close of my pants as she bites her lip in response and whispers, "You're going to blow my mind, aren't you?"

I grin in response and set to work, kissing every inch of her gorgeous pussy, moaning and licking and adding my fingers into the mix—fucking her with my hand as I flick my tongue back and forth across her clit, her every gasp and moan making me want her more. By the time she arches into my mouth, coming with a sexy cry that shreds the last of my self-control, I'm ready to sell my soul to be inside her.

But I don't have to give away anything precious to get what I need. This isn't a sacrifice. It's not a compromise.

Because Olivia wants me every bit as madly as I want her.

"Please, yes, please," she chants as I shed the rest of my clothing as fast as humanly possible and fumble in the headboard's drawer for a condom. "Please." She sneezes, making both of us laugh as I rip the package open. "Yes, yes." Another sneeze, another giggle and then we're coming together.

I push inside her and joy—pure and sweet and sexy— swells in my chest, making my heart ache as I begin to move inside my girl. My Olivia. My sunshine. My hope. My future.

"Crazy about you, Liv," I murmur against her lips as she wraps her long legs around me and holds on tight.

"You feel like a dream." She hums into my mouth. "And I don't ever want to wake up. Make love to me forever?"

"Forever," I promise, and as the lightning flashes and the wind wails through the trees outside, I do my best to keep my word.

But of course, no man can last forever, no matter how hard he's falling.

I thrust inside her, whispering promises, burying myself deep while she kisses and strokes me and sets my skin on fire, my body on fire, my soul on fire with her gasps and pleas and her very essence.

"Jace, yes, please," she moans, and my name on her lips drives me right to the edge.

"Liv," I cry. "Come for me, Sunshine."

Her head arches back, and as the first pulses of her climax wrap around me and hold tight, I release into her body's embrace with her name on my lips and her spirit dancing with mine. We come hard and deep—together, so right, so perfect, so *easy*, tumbling without a parachute, but we don't need one, because love has given us wings.

As the last waves of pleasure ebb away with the thunderstorm, we curl together on the bed, I pull her into my arms, and I hold her. Just...hold her. And it's perfect.

Nothing in my life has ever been easy.

But this?

Olivia, in my life, in my bed, and in my heart? She's the puzzle piece that *fits* after a lifetime of trying to put a corner piece into the center of the map.

"Love you," I whisper into the dark, after we've taken turns with the toothbrush beside the small sink, I've bolted down a giant glass of water, and we've fallen back into bed to let the storm lull us to sleep.

"Love, love, love you too," she sighs. "So that works out."

"It does," I agree, kissing the top of her head with a smile. And I keep smiling, right until the moment I slip into sleep and dream of the incredible woman in my arms.

TWENTY-ONE

Jace

Despite the giant glass of water I pounded before bed, I wake up with a cotton mouth and a crick in my neck. Still, considering how much I drank yesterday, it should be so much worse.

But somehow I got lucky...

I prop up on one arm, gazing down at Olivia's sleeping face and call it—yep. I'm the luckiest bastard in the world. She's so beautiful. So fucking perfect. With her full lips softly parted and her blond hair spread out across the pillow, she looks like an angel. Or a fairy-tale princess, waiting for her prince to climb the castle walls and kiss her awake.

"Give me three minutes," I whisper, pressing soft lips to her forehead.

Her lashes flutter, but she doesn't wake up, which is good. I want another glass of water and a close encounter with that toothbrush we found last night before I kiss her on the mouth again. But after that I'm going to give her the full prince treatment—from wake-up kisses to the slaying of any dragons that dare try to come between us.

It's all so clear now. I can't imagine how I deluded myself into thinking I could marry Ginger.

We'll work together to be good parents to our child, but in every other way, Ginger is my past. Olivia is my present and my future. Ginger was a decision made by a kid who secretly feared he'd never be good enough for anyone. Olivia is a choice made by a man who knows that he has a lot to give, and that he's finally found a woman with a heart big enough to accept all of it, all of *him*. And I'm ready for all of her too, every precious and irreplaceable piece.

Heart so full it feels like I'm slopping love over the edges onto the floor as I slip out of bed, I step quickly into my tux pants and dress shoes and cross to the door, curious to see how the forest fared in the storm. I open it to reveal devastation and a mud river rolling slowly by our front door in the watery morning light.

There are two trees down, the fire pit outside is filled with sludge, and Olivia's Vespa…

Her Vespa is gone.

I curse as I hurry down the steps. The mud sucks at my shoes, threatening to drag them off my feet, and I curse again. I have no idea how deep we are in the woods— having been unconscious most of the journey—but we've got to be at least a few miles from town. There wasn't a speck of light outside last night when I checked the windows before falling asleep, or any other sign of civiliza- tion. It's going to be a long, soggy trek back to Happy Cat if we have to do it on foot. Not to mention that Olivia loves that scooter. Or that she and Princess are too fucking cute when they go cruising for the sight of them in their matching head scarves to be stolen from the people of Georgia forever.

Hopefully it hasn't been carried too far away.

Keeping to higher ground, I follow the sludge down the hill and around a corner to a pile of brush someone must have cleared before building the she shed. And there, tangled in soggy branches is the Vespa, still in one piece, though decidedly dirtier than the last time I saw it. Wading into the mud, I manage to drag it out and get it upright on a patch of drier ground, but when I try to start it by turning the ignition key and hopping on the kick starter, it only makes a glugging sound, grumbles twice, and goes quiet.

I scoop out the sidecar with my hands as I ponder the problem. The scooter definitely got wet, but the sidecar seemed to take most of the soaking. I check the fuel petcock to make sure it's in the open position—it is—so that's not the issue. Could be some water in the exhaust pipe that needs to be blown out.

I try again, making sure to pull the choke out a little farther as I hop on the kick starter once, twice—causing more gurgling, bubbling noises from the back of the scooter —and on the third time a watery pop fills the air and it rumbles to life.

Grinning, I let the motor purr for few moments before shutting it off again.

Victory is mine.

Swiping my muddy hands on my tux pants—looks like I'll be buying this rental after all I've put it through—I head back up the rise, whistling softly in the increasingly warm, sunny morning. It's going to be another steamy summer day, perfect for jumping off the old bridge on my parents' property into the swimming hole below. After all the rain, our childhood spot will be muddy, but deep, clearing the bold jumper for somersaults and backflips.

Suddenly, I can't wait to show it to Olivia. To hold her hand and take a wild leap.

To show off my backflip like I'm sixteen again because that's the way she makes me feel. Young, crazy in the best way, and more alive than I can remember feeling in so damned long. I jog the last ten feet to the shed, so excited to see her that when I throw open the door and find the bed empty, my brain refuses to believe my eyes.

"Olivia?" I call, even though there's nowhere for her to hide in the tiny love shack. Even the toilet—a composting number behind a circular curtain in the corner—isn't totally private. The floor below the curtain is completely visible, and there are no elegant Olivia toes in sight.

Maybe she went outside? To look for me?

But even as I turn to head back outside, my gut insists that's not what happened. My gut warns that the covers wouldn't be on the floor if Olivia had just stepped outside to see where I'd gotten off to. That the violet that was perched on the windowsill when we came in would still be in its spot, soaking up the morning sun, not turned over on the ground, spilling soil onto the rainbow-colored rug.

That violet wasn't on the ground when I left....

Was it? I was so distracted by the rest of the storm devastation, I can't remember, but I don't think it was and I can't imagine Olivia walking by the overturned flower and not stopping to put it right again.

I shouldn't have gone looking for her Vespa until she woke up. What if she's out searching for me, getting sucked into a mud pit?

Outside on the small porch, I call her name again, my voice echoing through the trees, but there's no response except the caw of a crow perched a dozen feet away.

A crow on top of an SUV with the sheriff's department shield emblazoned on the side.

Fuck. Fuck, fuck, fuck…

Cops, in my experience, are never good news, and I'm not naïve enough to believe that this time will be any different.

"Jace O'Dell, you're under arrest." The nasal drawl sounds from my left and I spin to see Chester circling around the shed, his handcuffs already off his utility belt and in hand.

My stomach plummets, but I refuse to go quietly. Not this time. Chester needs to get the message that he can't fuck with me for his own entertainment anymore. "I don't think so, Rotten. I haven't done anything wrong, and I'm done putting up with your bullshit."

"So you want to add resisting arrest to the charges." He shrugs, barely concealing the grin tugging at his lips. "Fine with me."

"To what charges? You don't have shit on me. I've been here, in this shed, with Olivia all night long. Whatever you think I did, I didn't do it, and I've got an air-tight alibi. She'll back me up. As soon as she gets here."

His smile goes ugly at the edges. "That's going to be hard for her to do, considering she's the reason I'm taking you in. You're under arrest for conspiracy to fake a kidnapping. Anything you say can and will be used against you in a court of law, so please, tell me you're done putting up with my bullshit again. I'm sure the judge is going to love hearing that you've got zero respect for law enforcement as well as zero respect for sweet, dim-witted girls too trusting to know better than to get involved in criminal schemes with losers like you."

A scowl claws at my forehead. "What the *fuck* are you talking about? We didn't fake a kidnapping. Where's Olivia? What did you do with her?"

He approaches me with that smarmy smile still

stretching his ugly lips. "Go on, O'Dell. Keep talking. Can't wait to tell the judge you confessed to everything. And tell Ginger too. That poor woman certainly deserves some answers after everything you've put her through."

I need to shut up. I know I need to shut up, because I've done this dance before. Resisting Chester the Ass-Festerer won't get me anywhere. But I want to run.

I want to run, and to find Olivia, and to figure out what the *fuck* is going on here.

"Go on, O'Dell," he hisses. "Make a break for it. I've been looking for an excuse to taser your ass for *years.*"

"No one kidnapped anyone," I grit out. "She fucking *saved* me."

"Then why do we have her confession on tape?"

What the *hell*? I was only gone twenty minutes. He can't have a confession on tape.

Something stinks worse than my breath. And I need to solve this.

I need to solve this and make sure Olivia's okay.

And I need to do it *now*. Whatever it takes.

TWENTY-TWO

Jace

I hate making these phone calls. But it's so routine, I don't even have to ask the booking officer if I can use my phone to look up Ryan's number, because I have it memorized.

So here I am, back in Happy Cat's holding cell, using my one call on a Saturday morning that was supposed to be the start of my new life with Olivia.

"Jace?" Ryan says, which kills me, because I haven't even opened my mouth to say *hi*.

Don't have to.

Because he's probably sitting at home, having breakfast with Cassie, and he knows what *Collect call from the Happy Cat jail, will you accept charges?* means.

"They said I faked my own kidnapping," I spit out. "They took my cell phone. Showed up in the middle of the woods and arrested me because I didn't get married last night. Fuck, *I* didn't even know where I was and they found me. Us. Me. *Shit*. Ryan. I don't know what the hell's going on, but you've gotta get me out of here."

"They said *what*?"

Outrage and disbelief. That, at least, is new, a very different tone from the one I'm used to hearing on one of these phone calls. Usually, when I call Ryan from jail, it's resigned support. *Yeah, I'm on my way, we'll figure this out, you little fuck-up.*

Of course, he never says that. He believes in me even when he shouldn't.

I just hope he believes in me today.

"Where's Olivia? Have you seen Olivia?" I ask, because it's impossible to think too much about anything else right now. "They said she confessed to being in on it, which is insane, because this wasn't a plan. We're being set up and I don't know why and I have to fix this, but I can't, because I'm sitting in jail for no fucking reason."

I need to shut up, because I know this is a recorded line, but my head hurts, my heart hurts, and I don't know where Olivia is.

She didn't sell me out to the cops.

Not Olivia.

No. Fucking. Way.

"Slow down, slow down," Ryan says. "Cassie—call Olivia. Okay, Jace, listen, we're going to sort this out. Do you need bail money?"

"They haven't set bail because it's *Saturday*. Judge isn't in until Monday. They're saying I have to stay here *all fucking weekend*. For a crime that I didn't commit. I've done a lot of shit to get myself in trouble, and yeah, I'll own it, but I didn't fake my own kidnapping. She *saved* me."

He curses beneath his breath. "You told them they've got it all wrong, right?"

"Chester," I grit out.

"*Dammit.*"

"Exactly."

He blows out an audible breath, then says something I can't hear. Probably talking to Cassie.

My booking officer taps her wristwatch. "Ryan, I'm running out of time. You have to get me out of here."

"We're on it, Jace. Just sit tight. Don't say a word. Not one fucking word. About anything. Understand?"

"Where's Olivia? Did Cassie get through to Olivia?"

"We're gonna sort this out, okay? Just hang tight. I'm tossing on some clothes and heading your way."

"Ryan—"

"*Hang. Tight. Mouth. Shut.*"

The phone beeps and goes dead, and my booking officer rises.

I've sent out the Bat Signal. Everything else is out of my hands now. I could try to break out of jail, but I did that once at seventeen and learned my lesson about how little the sheriff's department appreciates my knack with lock picking. If I want to sort my life out with Olivia and Ginger and the baby, I have to sit tight.

I fucking *hate* sitting tight.

And *fuck*.

Ginger.

I wonder if anyone's told Ginger I was arrested. What kind of mood she'll be in today. How pissed she is at me.

She should be pissed.

I bailed on her. And lied to her.

But she's lied to me too, dammit. She doesn't love me. Or if she does, not the way Olivia loves me. Olivia's love is kind and good-intentioned. She's a top-notch human being in every way. She adopts random hedgehogs and stuffed squirrels and worries about balancing other peoples' energy fields and saving the planet. Ginger has an asshole pedigreed show cat that pukes in my shoes. She flirts with other guys to make me jealous and reminds me that I'm a fuck-up with few redeeming qualities, aside from my long and talented dick, every chance she gets.

Ginger and I have definitely done enough uncool things to each other for me to say we're even, call a truce, and move forward without any lingering wedding-ditching guilt hanging over my head. For the good of *both* of us. And the baby.

And Olivia...

God, I just need to know she's okay.

"I didn't do it," I rasp out to the deputy.

She doesn't answer.

She doesn't have to.

She's heard it from criminals too many times to believe it.

"I want to talk to the sheriff," I tell her.

She sighs. "He's out till Monday too."

Fuck.

Just *fuck*.

I'm so tired of my entire life being fucked.

Hang in there, Olivia, I think, hoping she can feel my vibes. *Wherever you are, I'm going to get there as fast as I can.*

TWENTY-THREE

Olivia

I'm a firm believer in karma. What you sow, you reap. What you put out into the universe comes back to you tenfold. If you make spiritually unwise decisions, sooner or later they *will* come back to bite you in the butt.

But I've never had karma take a chomp out of me quite this quickly before.

Less than twenty-four hours after my first kidnapping — and hopefully my *only* kidnapping, it's not something I want to make a habit of doing on a regular basis — I have gone from kidnapper to kidnappee.

But my kidnap destination is much less pleasant than a cozy she shed in the heart of the woods.

It is, in fact, downright creepy.

"Please, Ginger, can't we talk about this?" I beg, hands lifted by my sides as I move deeper into the abandoned gymnasium.

"Keep walking," she snaps, shoving me to keep me moving. "Say another word before we get to the office and the little pig gets it."

Ginger tightens her grip on Princess's tiny throat and the sweet baby squeals in pain, making my heart lurch and tears spring to my eyes. If she hurts my little girl, I'm not sure what I'm going to do. I'm a pacifist who's always stood behind my belief that an eye for an eye makes the whole world blind.

But a person who terrifies and tortures defenseless hedgehogs doesn't deserve eyes. Or fingers. Or anything else they can use to inflict suffering on the innocent.

"Fine, I'm going," I cry out. "I'm going, please just… stop hurting her."

"*You're* hurting her. Cut the crap and your pet will be fine. Keep fucking with me and we're going to have problems." Ginger's features pucker at the center of her pale face, making her look like a piece of fruit that's started to go rotten at the core. She's still wearing her wedding dress, a gorgeous, white poof of a thing with a princess bodice and long flowing skirt, with her hair as flawlessly arranged as it was yesterday, when she almost got married, but there's nothing beautiful about her.

Her aura is an ugly green and purple bruise filled with energetic puss. She isn't beyond help—no one is, we can all turn our energetic lives around at any time—but she's miles down a bad road, one that leads to suffering for her and all the things she holds dear.

I want to beg her to turn around. To let me go. To make this right before it's too late.

But I already tried all that on the way here, after she forced me into the driver's seat of her Jetta at hedgehog-point and made me drive back through Happy Cat, past the Wild Hog and the rental homes by the railroad tracks, back behind the town electrical station to a group of buildings tucked into the edge of the woods by the river that I've never seen before.

The sign on the outside of the tornado-damaged compound of red and gray metal buildings reads Happy Clown Circus School, but there's nothing happy left in this place. The springy tumbling floor I pass by on my way through the main room lets off a pungent, moldy odor, the trampoline stretched over a concrete pit in the corner has a gash ripped down the middle, and above us the remnants of a damaged trapeze sway eerily in the breeze creeping in through the shattered windows.

But most disturbingly, there are clowns...

Clown-sized footprints painted on the floor, clown costumes hanging on the wall, and a giant clown mural on the far wall that makes my skin crawl as I move into its energy field. It's a painting of a male clown with his head thrown back, laughing so hard tears are streaming down his painted cheeks, with his mouth open wide enough to see his fillings. But he doesn't look happy. He looks like he's in pain, like he's being tortured by his own laughter.

I want to pass through the doorway beneath his tear-streaked cheek about as much as I want to gorge myself on unethically raised meat products full of antibiotics and hormones, but I have to keep going. Princess's safety depends on it.

I enter a shadowy corridor with several doors on either side and stiff, dusty, plastic chairs along the wall. It reminds me of the principal's office at my high school in California.

After years of being homeschooled or tutored with the other kids on the set of Savannah's TV show before it finally ended its run, I was unprepared for a normal ninth grade experience. I spent hours sitting outside the principal's office for the sins of going to the bathroom without a pass, asking the teacher too many questions, or taking a stray dog I found outside the cafeteria to the animal shelter without having a parent check me out for the day.

I wasn't good at following the rules and it got me in trouble.

And this is the same thing all over again. I broke the rules, and now I'm going to pay for it. But how much? What price does Ginger think is fair to pay for ruining her wedding?

When we first got in the car, I thought she just wanted to get me away from Jace before he came back to the shed, but now...

"What are we doing here, Ginger?" I ask, voice trembling as we shuffle deeper into the shadows of the unlit passage. "This is crazy. There's no way this ends well for you or me or anyone else. Just let me go and I promise I won't tell anyone."

"There. Third door on the left. Open it." She huffs, so close to me now that I can feel her breath between my shoulder blades. "Today, blondie. If I don't get over to visit Jace in jail, he's going to think I'm still mad about the wedding."

I turn, a frown burrowing into my forehead. "Jail? What on earth? Why would—"

"You're opening the door, not asking questions. Do it! Now!" She squeezes Princess so tight my baby starts squirming madly, her tiny eyes wide with terror and pitiful whimpers keening through the air.

"You're a monster," I shout, the words bursting from my chest with a sob as she kicks one heeled slipper in the air, gesturing to the door with her foot.

"Inside! Now!"

I fumble for the door, tears making her face swim as I tumble into a musty room and immediately start sneezing. I sneeze and sneeze and sneeze again, so hard my nose starts to ache and my ears to ring. By the time I recover, it's too late to investigate my surroundings or to beg Ginger to leave Princess with me. She's already slamming the door, the creaking and banging noises indicating she's wedging a chair or something under the handle. When she's done, she flips me the bird through the small window above the broken desk against the wall.

"Now sit there and think about what you've done," she says, holding a still-squirming Princess up to the window. "And just in case you think it's a good idea to try to get out, remember I've got your rodent. If I come back and you're not here, the little shit gets it."

"No, please! Come back!" I cry out, hurrying to the window and placing my hands on the thick glass. But she is already storming away down the hall, taking my hedgehog with her, proving I can't protect any of the creatures I love.

Now Ginger's got Princess and she's on her way back to town to Jace, who's apparently in jail for some reason, and I'm trapped here in…

Where exactly am I trapped?

I turn, taking in my prison, my heart stuttering to a stop as I lay eyes on the monstrosity in the corner.

It's a giant stuffed teddy bear. Dressed as a clown.

It's missing one eye, has stuffing spilling out of its neck like someone tried to chop its head off, but died trying, and as I watch, the belly…ripples beneath the tight polka dot tee shirt it's wearing. It squirms and bumps and then there's a scratching sound, one that makes it clear something is living inside the bear, something with claws that is probably hungry.

Maybe hungry enough to decide a human finger or toe sounds like a good snack.

I remember hearing stories about rats eating the fingers

of prisoners in dungeons in the Middle Ages and in poor houses in London in the 1800s and the room begins to spin. Then my mind starts pulling up other terrifying rodent facts —that their teeth never stop growing and that they really can swim up through your toilet and that they're responsible for the Black Death that wiped out almost fifty percent of the population of Europe—and the whirling gets worse.

And then the giant teddy bear lurches suddenly to one side, wrenched from his rest by the critters living in his guts, and I'm a goner. My knees buckle and the world goes black as I sink to the floor with one final sneeze.

TWENTY-FOUR

Jace

I want to punch my fist through Chester's face.

I want it more than I want The Back Door to bring back their old wing sauce recipe or for the Braves to win the World Series.

But I don't want it more than I want Olivia back in my arms.

So even though my knuckles are itching and my fingers aching to ball up and pop that lying, crooked sack of shit in the mouth, I'm sitting here in the sheriff's office keeping my mouth shut and letting Ryan do the talking.

Mostly.

"Clearly a misunderstanding," Ryan's saying, because he and Sheriff Briggs are chums, what with Ryan being a fire-fighter and all. He's one of the *good* guys, and even Briggs, who also has a stick up his ass most days, can't help liking my perfect big brother. "You have his phone. Which he left on, knowing that Ginger had him on her Phone Friends app and could track him down at any time. Doesn't seem like the behavior of a man who was trying to hide from the sheriff after orchestrating some kind of fake kidnapping conspiracy. So why are you holding him exactly? What evidence do you have?"

The sheriff eyes me, then Chester, who puffs up his chest. "The entire town of Happy Cat saw him being abducted from his wedding."

I clench my jaw to keep from yelling that I went willingly.

"I can promise you he wasn't abducted. Either for real or as part of some elaborate plan," Ryan says dryly. "Olivia just showed up. And he went willingly. Simple as that."

"See?" Chester says triumphantly. "They admit he was a part of it."

"No, we admit he didn't want to get married," Ryan says. "Not getting married isn't a crime."

"It should be," Chester mutters. "And why did Olivia Moonbeam leave town if she wasn't an accessory to a crime?"

Briggs chews on his moustache and looks at me. "Right. Why did Olivia Moonbeam leave town? And where is she?"

Is he fucking kidding? "She didn't leave town."

"Your proof?"

"Sheriff, my girlfriend went over to Olivia's house as soon as Jace called me this morning," Ryan interjects. "The lock on the door was broken and her hedgehog is missing."

Fuck. Fuck fuck *fuck.* "Princess is gone? You didn't tell me that."

"Proves she left town," Chester pipes up. "She's not the type to leave without her pet."

"And the broken lock?" Ryan asks, still remarkably calm.

"Must have lost her keys." Chester shrugs.

The sheriff harumphs. "You said you got a phone call, Chester. One you taped. Where is that?"

Chester's skin goes mottled under his smarmy eyes. "I… it's processing."

The sheriff scowls. "Processing?"

"It's on the way," Chester insists. "I'll have it soon."

The sheriff's scowl becomes a full-fledged glower of disapproval. "You arrested Jace without due process?"

"I…heard it. On my phone," he blusters. "But I didn't record the line. But someone else did. I'm picking it up later today. He's a known criminal, Sheriff. It was in everyone's best interest to pick him up fast, before he skipped town completely."

"Who has the tape?" Ryan asks.

"Witnesses are confidential," Chester sniffs.

"Swear to god, you—" I start, but Ryan grips my arm and yanks.

Hard.

"Sheriff, you're releasing Jace right now," Ryan says firmly.

There's no threat in his voice, but he doesn't have to issue threats.

Ryan's popular.

The sheriff's elected. After the barest beat of hesitation, he pins me with a hard look. "Don't leave town. You're a material witness in a potential crime. Understood?"

"He understands, Sheriff." Ryan grips me by the back of the collar and lifts, and I stand with him. "His belongings? And you'll send someone over to check out Olivia's house, won't you?"

Twenty minutes later, I'm being shown out of the sheriff's office. I don't so much as turn my head when I pass Chester's desk and he mutters, "Don't get too comfortable on the outside, O'Dell. You're still a criminal, and you'll always be a criminal."

"Hush," a female deputy I don't recognize whispers to Chester as Ryan and I pass by. "Innocent until proven guilty, Chess. Now where's Quillie Nelson? I brought the bandana with the braids attached that I made for him. I can't wait to see it on!"

From the corner of my eye, I see Chester pull a cage out from under his desk.

A cage with a hedgehog in it who is the spitting image of Princess von Spooksalot.

Who is not at Olivia's house.

Which was broken into.

I almost stop to demand where he got the hedgehog and call him a lying bastard, but think better of it and keep my feet pointed toward the exit. Chester's not going to give me a straight answer about anything. Ever. And it doesn't take much mulling to come to the conclusion that Chester could be the son of a bitch who stole Princess, making it look like Olivia ran off instead of being taken.

I knew that fucker had it out for me.

I also know Olivia wouldn't disappear, just like I know she wouldn't call in a report that we cooked up a fake kidnapping scheme.

Someone took her and Chester helped them and now he's got Princess in a cage dressed as Willie Nelson and the world is going to hell in a fucking handbasket.

If one quill on that hedgehog's body is harmed when I'm finally able to prove it, I'm going to beat the shit out of Chester, consequences be damned.

Outside in the waiting room, Cassie, Blake, and Hope are all waiting on the benches along the wall. When they see Ryan and me, they surge to their feet, swarming us as we head for the door.

"Outside," I mutter, glancing over my shoulder at the woman at the front desk. "I don't want to talk in here."

"Good idea," Cassie says.

We push out into the muggy day, and I immediately start to sweat in the noon sun, making me wonder again where Olivia is. Hopefully she's somewhere cool and relatively safe. In this heat, if the kidnapper left her in a car or trunk, she could be dead within a few hours.

The thought makes my stomach jerk as I step into the shade of the elm trees at the base of the steps and turn to face my family. And Hope. Somehow I've acquired an entourage, but I'm grateful for every one of them.

The more people searching for Olivia, the better.

"I think Chester has Princess," I say, making eye contact with each member of my posse. "I just saw him pull a cage with a hedgehog in it out from under his desk. And if he took Princess to make it look like Olivia ran off, I wouldn't be surprised to learn he was the one who took her too. Or had a buddy of his do it. She was there, and then she wasn't, and the only person out there was Chester. He's involved, I'm fucking sure of it."

"He doesn't have any buddies. He's the worst." Cassie's forehead furrows in sympathy. "But he didn't take Princess."

"How do you know?" I ask. "It's not like he's going to tell the truth."

She casts a guilty look Ryan's way. "I may have heard through the grapevine that Chester had a hedgie, and I may have heard that he brought his pet into the sheriff's office today, and I may have talked someone into showing us that Quillie Nelson was a boy."

"And he's definitely a boy," Hope says, making my

spirits sink lower. "He's also pedigreed and registered as a hedge breeding stud with Chester listed as his owner for the past two years. He carries the paperwork with him, and it checks out. But I still think Chester's lying about something. I can smell it on him."

"Or that might have been the sour yogurt you 'accidentally' spilled all over the jacket hanging on the back of his chair," Blake says without looking at her.

Hope bobs a shoulder. "What? It was an accident."

"Basically, they're lucky they both weren't arrested," Ryan says dryly.

Cassie wrinkles her nose. "We were polite. Mostly."

Ryan wraps an arm around her shoulders, hugging her close to his side. "It's all right. We've all wanted to call Chester out at one point or another."

"He totally deserves that and more," Hope says, heat in her tone. "He's a horrible parent. Quillie hasn't been socialized properly. He's a cranky little biter. Just like his owner."

Blake shakes his head with a roll of his eyes.

"What?" Hope crosses her arms at her chest, glaring up at him. "Chester bites. That has been proven by multiple eye witness accounts."

"In kindergarten," Blake replies. "I don't like him either, but I don't think we can judge a grown man by what he did when he was six years old. If we did, I'd still be eating play dough and seeing if I could get a spaghetti noodle to go in through one nostril and out through the other."

"So his hedgehog is a biter," I interrupt, because God only knows how long these two could go at it if we let them. "Does that mean he'd be aggressive with a mate if he had one?"

Hope lifts her honeyed brown eyes to mine. "Sure. I'm not an expert on hedgehogs by any means, but I've done a lot of reading since Olivia brought Princess home. It sounds like males and females usually shouldn't be caged together except during the actual mating process. Kind of like humans." She laughs, then winces and shakes her head. "Sorry. My parents fought all the time. Dysfunctional family joke, not appropriate with a friend missing."

Cassie rests a hand between her shoulders. "Don't worry about it. We all deal with stress in our ways. I poke people in the stomach. And I have a very sharp finger."

"So Chester could have been the one who abandoned Princess in the park," I say, chewing on the inside of my lip. "And if he was, then he might have seen Olivia and me together."

"Didn't Chester have a thing for Ginger back in high school?" Blake says.

I nod. "There wasn't anything he wouldn't do for her. All she had to do was crook a finger and he'd come running, even though he didn't have a chance with her, but she'd always give him something else to keep his loyalty. We used to fight about it all the time. So if he saw me kissing Olivia, then he probably followed us, which is why he was in the right place at the right time to arrest George and me for taking a piss in public. And he would've told Ginger about all of it, even though we were broken up. And if he was mad enough on Ginger's behalf to arrest me for kissing another woman, then I imagine he'd be pretty damned pissed at the woman who ruined Ginger's wedding. Maybe pissed enough to make her disappear?"

"You sure he'd still do that for her?" Hope asks. "Because I kinda got the impression he was into Olivia. Not that he was Ginger's lackey."

I shake my head. "Once you start doing shit for Ginger, you don't stop. She's…"

"Irresistible?" Blake suggests.

"Persuasive," I sigh. The woman knows how to hit where it hurts.

And how many times has she brought me back by reminding me that no one else would want my sorry ass?

"But if he is into Olivia... What if he saw this as a convenient opportunity to convince her there could be something between them..." Cassie says softly, and my balls shrivel up.

"So we start sneaking around Chester's house and go from there." I clasp my hands and rub the heels of my palms together, about to jump out of my skin with the need to do something to find Olivia. Especially if she's in danger.

Ryan growls. "No. *You* do not."

"But what if he's right?" Blake asks, while Hope and Cassie nod along. "Olivia's missing. We all know she wouldn't have left town. Where would she even go?"

"Chester's in hot water at the moment," Ryan says firmly. "We can start looking for her while we wait for Sheriff Briggs to check out her house and find this supposed tape of Olivia ratting you out. But you, Jace, are not going to be the one snooping around Chester's. Otherwise, you *will* be in jail until Monday."

"But I can't stand this," I say. "I have going to go look for her. Now." I lift my hands in surrender to Ryan. "Yes, I'll stay away from Chester's, but I have to look somewhere." I turn to Blake, poking him in the shoulder. "Take me home. I need my truck."

After calling in reinforcements in the form of Ruthie May, Maud and Gerald, and some other trusted friends, we split up, each group claiming the part of town where they'll focus their search.

I am, of course, once again ordered to keep my nose clean.

And I will. But only because I can't search for Olivia if I'm in jail.

"Don't do anything stupid," Blake says when he pulls into my driveway around the side of my house and cuts the engine.

"When have I ever done something stupid?" I reach for the handle, but he stops me with a hand on my arm.

"At least tell me where you're really going to look so I can back you up if I need to. And so I can make sure you're not anywhere near Chester."

"I'm going where I said I was going. Out to The Kennedy School and the shops around there. It's the closest sign of civilization to where Olivia and I were staying in the woods. Seriously, I don't want to end up in jail. I'm going to keep my nose clean."

He nods. "Okay. I'll be downtown, not far from the bar. Call if you need anything."

"Thanks," I say, my throat tight. "I can't shake the feeling that if we don't find her soon something terrible is going to happen. Or maybe…" I trail off, the words in my head too awful to repeat aloud.

"We'll find her," he says softly. "And she'll be okay until we do. She's tougher than we gave her credit for, you know. Takes a pretty ballsy woman to snatch a guy from his own wedding."

He pops a grin that makes me feel more confident that he's right. That we'll find her.

"I'm so glad she did." I take a deep breath and let it out slow. "I don't love Ginger anymore. Not even a little. I'm totally gone on Olivia."

"Duh, man." Blake smiles. "Called it a while ago. Glad you finally figured it out though. Before you had to take Ginger to divorce court." He glances over my shoulder, his gaze hardening as his mouth goes tight at the edges. "Speak of the devil…"

I glance over my shoulder, stomach lurching as I see Ginger emerging from her car in front of the house and rushing up the steps to the porch, still in her wedding dress.

Fuck.

Part of me wants to dive for my truck, since she clearly hasn't seen us sitting here on the side of the house.

The other part of me knows it's past time to take care of this. But *now*? When Olivia's missing?

I'll tell her any damn thing she wants to hear today to get her out of my way.

"Want me to stay for moral support?" Blake asks.

"No. I want you to start looking. I'll get rid of Ginger, change out of this damned tux, and text you as soon as I'm on the move." I open the door, hopping out before I toss my next words over my shoulder. "Call me if you find anything. Anything at all."

"Will do. Good luck."

I have a feeling we're going to need more than luck, but I'll take anything the universe is willing to throw my way.

TWENTY-FIVE

Jace

I slam the door and Blake starts up his truck, backing out as I jog around the side of the house to the porch.

Ginger comes flying down the steps before I get there.

"Oh my god! Are you okay? I've been worried sick," she says, her bloodshot eyes finding mine as she clutches at the front of my dress shirt. Her dress is still immaculate, though a little wrinkled, making me think she must have slept in it. "I tried to visit you at the jail but they said you'd already been let go. And thank god, right?" She laughs, high and piercing. "I can't believe that hippie nutjob kidnapped you. But you're okay, now, right, Jacey?"

I cover her hands with mine, gently, but deliberately pulling them away from my shirt, and start walking her down the steps. "It's okay. I'm fine. Obviously, we need to talk, about a lot of things, but I can't right now."

She blinks so fast her head twitches back and forth.

"What? What are you even talking about? Of course we need to talk *right now*. A crazy person ruined our wedding, Jace. I didn't know where you were for an entire night. You could have been hurt or—"

"I wasn't hurt," I cut her off, but tread lightly. One wrong word, and she'll be staging a sit-in at my house to keep me from leaving. "I was—listen, Ginger, I didn't sleep well last night, and I had an awful morning. I'm sorry you were worried, but right now, I really need to get some sleep."

Her jaw drops and her bottom lip trembles. "You were with her last night, weren't you? While I'm here pregnant with our child, you were *with her*."

"Ginger—"

"She's just a dumb blond from California, for god's sake. She doesn't belong here. She doesn't know you the way I know you, she doesn't—"

"She's not dumb," I insist, pushing on before she can get started again. I'm not going back there with her, to the same place we've always gone. "Ginger. Listen. This isn't about her or me or you, and I need some time and space to come to my senses."

There.

That sounds like something she'd say to me, things she *has* said to me in the past when she wanted to win an argument, whether it was over breaking up, staying together, or her flirting right in front of me to get me jealous.

"You were with her on our *wedding night*, Jace?" She shakes her head, sending tears streaming down her pale cheeks. "Of course you need some time to come to your senses. Baby, being scared of marriage is normal, but we're meant to be. We've been meant to be since high school. Who else would've stood by you through all the troubles you've had? Who else? No one. But me? I'm not going anywhere."

Jaw clenched, I draw a hand through my epic bed head —a night in a shed, followed by a morning in jail has left me looking as rough as I feel.

And she's doing it again.

She's using my past against me in a way Olivia never would, feeding me the same lines, except this time, I realize the lines aren't because she loves me, but because she wants to *own* me.

Clearly, getting through to her is going to be a bigger job than I thought, one I don't have the time or energy for today. "We can talk more later." I move around her, starting toward the front porch. "I've really got to get going."

"Where? To look for her?" Ginger's voice catches on a sob. "You're not going to find her. Chester said she probably left town."

Suspicion hooks in my chest and I spin slowly around, playing it cool, because when the *fuck* did she talk to Chester? And *why*? And if she talked to Chester, why the *fuck* was I arrested for *conspiracy to fake a kidnapping*? "He did?"

She nods fast. "Yes! He said her hedgehog was gone and some of her clothes from her dresser too. She probably got scared she was going to get arrested for kidnapping and ran away. Which means she doesn't love you, Jace. If she did, she would have been there when you got back from digging her stupid scooter out of the mud."

I press my lips together, pretending to consider her words, while my thoughts race.

There's a chance Chester could have told her about the scooter—surely he saw it when he was poking around the shed—but my gut tells me its more than that. My gut is screaming that Ginger isn't relaying something she heard

186 PIPPA GRANT & LILI VALENTE

secondhand. She's talking about something she saw. Because she was *there*, helping Chester take Olivia.

Or maybe just doing the job herself.

So Chester could take *me*?

Why the hell would Ginger be talking to Chester so much if she isn't in on whatever scheme he's playing?

My hands curl into fists at my sides as I imagine how it went down—did Ginger use a gun? Or maybe something held over Olivia's face while she was sleeping to knock her out before she dragged the woman I love into her car?—but I refuse to let my suspicions show on my face. Instead, I sigh again, and rub at the skin above my eyes. "I don't know, Ginger. I'm too wrecked to talk right now. Honestly, I can barely keep my eyes open. The last couple days have been a whirlwind."

"You poor thing," she coos, wrapping her fingers around my forearm. "That woman's been playing you hard, and she has you all confused and exhausted. But she left you, honey. I know that's hard to hear, but it's the truth."

I furrow my brow. "I don't know what the truth is right now. But I know I probably shouldn't drive. At least not until I get some rest."

"You need a nap." She bounces lightly on her toes, like a nap is the most exciting thing she's talked about in years. "We could take one together! I'll make you a sandwich and then we can shower, pull the shades, and take a nice long nap in the air conditioning. It's too hot to be outside right now anyway. And when you wake up, your head will be clear. You'll see."

"Maybe," I say, knowing I can't change my tune too fast or she'll get suspicious. And I can't let her stay here. I need her to leave.

So I can follow her.

"But I'm not up for company." I shift my arm, twisting out of her grasp. "I need to be alone. To rest and...to think."

"Are you sure?" Ginger watches me cross to the porch, her eyebrows twitching in an upside down V. "I could just sit quietly in the kitchen. Have some tea while you sleep? That way I'll be there when you wake up."

Shit, I have *got* to get rid of her.

"Ginger, I'm not going to get my head straight with you on top of me. I need space. But I'll call you the minute I wake up, okay?"

"You better." Her voice is semi-flirty, but her eyes are spelling danger as her hands drift down to her belly. "Because you *know* what's at stake, right, Jacey?"

Fuck. *Fuck.* "Yes, Ginger. I know what's at stake. And I *will* call you. The minute I wake up."

Which will be a long damned time, because I'm not sleeping until I've found Olivia.

"Okay. Good." Her fingers tangle together. "Talk soon. I'll miss you!"

I lift a hand, waving goodbye as I climb the steps, feigning weariness until I'm inside the house with the door shut behind me. Then I launch into motion, tearing off my dress shirt and tux pants as I race to the laundry room beside the kitchen. I drag on jeans and a tee shirt and grab my tennis shoes from the rack beside the door, pulling them on with one hand as I peek through the blinds with the other.

Ginger's in her car, but she hasn't left yet. Perfect.

I shove my phone in my pocket, grab my wallet and keys and make a run for the back door, circling around to where my truck is parked beside the house just as she rumbles away down the gravel road, driving too fast, getting dust on Blake's grapes the way she always does. But

I've got bigger things to worry about than a bitch session from my baby brother.

Ginger's been talking to Chester.

Ginger hates Olivia as much as Chester hates me.

I'll need to figure out what to do about Ginger and the baby, but if she's in on this—if she's hurt Olivia—then not even Sheriff Briggs will be able to argue that I'm not the better parent.

And if Ginger took Olivia, there's a chance she'll be headed to wherever she's locked her up.

Assuming she's trapped Olivia somewhere and not killed her and tossed her body off a bridge.

The thought makes my hands shake as I start up the truck and pull out. Ginger's crazy, but she's not a killer. She's the kind of person who slips artificial sweetener into your cake and lies about it being the real thing, not a psycho who fills the sugar bowl with arsenic.

At least, that's what I have to believe.

As I pull down the drive, following Ginger close, but not too close, hoping to stay off her radar, I tell myself a hundred times that Olivia is okay. She's okay and soon she's going to be even better. Because soon, she's going to be back in my arms, where I will keep her safe from anyone or anything that tries to hurt her—crooked cops, crazy ex-girl-friends, or anyone else stupid enough to come after the woman I love.

And God help anyone who tries to stand in my way.

TWENTY-SIX

Olivia

I wake up aching like I've been sleeping on a bed of rocks and moan, wondering if someone messed up the Dr Pepper again and I passed out in my flowerbed with the garden gnomes. All my gnomes are made of stone and not very comfortable bedmates, as I discovered the time I decided to roll around in the jasmine during the new moon and absorb the flowers' anxiety-relieving vibes.

But the moment my eyes flicker open, it all comes rushing back—the kidnapping, Jace, the hedgehog abuse, and the giant teddy bear clown monster with the finger-chomping rats in its belly.

I sit up fast, gulping as I lift my hands in front of my face, relieved to see eight fingers and two thumbs, just like when I passed out.

Passed out…

Oh my god, I passed out. And I must have been out for

a while, judging by the snarling sensation in my stomach and the angle of the sunlight streaming down the hall. But though it's warm and sticky in here, I'm still in one piece and a glance at the bear reveals that all is quiet on the tummy front. In reality, whatever's living in there is probably just as scared of me as I am of it. Most animals just want to be left in peace, they don't actually want to hurt anyone.

Unlike human beings…

The thought brings me to my feet and crossing to the door to try the handle. Ginger said she'd hurt Princess if I tried to escape, but I have to try anyway. Ginger isn't in her right mind and people who are that out of harmony with reality are dangerous. If she snaps out of it, she could come back feeling sorry for what she's done and set me free. Or she could come back even more deluded than she was before and decide to hurt me, maybe even kill me. And I know Princess wouldn't want me to risk it. She'd want me to try to save myself, even if it put her in danger, because she's a brave and honorable hedgehog.

And hopefully, once I'm gone, Ginger will see that hurting Princess is pointless.

And Jace too.

Jace.

Where is he? Did they take him?

I have to get out. I have to get to the sheriff and hopefully they'll be able to rescue everyone.

"Please, please, please," I mutter as I tug and push and tug on the door, but it's no use. Ginger must have wedged the chair on the other side in tight.

With a huff of frustration, I shift my attention to the window. It's thick and crisscrossed with tiny threads of some sort of metal—copper maybe?—embedded in the glass. It looks pretty sturdy, but I might be able to break it, if I can find something hard enough.

I turn, scanning the room, seeing things I didn't notice before, now that I'm able to concentrate on something aside from the giant teddy clown. There are other toys stored in here too. Along the wall to my left are shelves lined with tin toys, some of which look old enough to be worth something to a collector. There are little tin robots and spaceships, tin wagons pulled by tin horses, and a multitude of tin clowns engaged in various clowning activities.

They're cute—and creepy—but none of them is big enough or heavy enough to shatter a window, so I keep looking.

On the floor beneath the shelves are two dusty canvas bins filled with brightly colored balls of various sizes—also not hard or hammer-like—and in the corner sits a rocking horse made of wood so old I'm pretty sure it would shatter on impact with the glass.

"Come on, we've got this," I mumble, funneling positive energy into my aura. "There has to be something."

A sneeze claws its way up to my nose in response, and I detonate, sneezing until my eyes are watering. I silently vow to visit an actual real live doctor as soon as I escape—anything to get this ridiculousness under control—and circle around the teddy bear, looking for treasure on the other side of the stuffy.

There I find bags of clown noses and hats and costumes, complete with huge clown shoes, which would be fantastic if I could scare the glass out of the window. But I can't, and the odds of the glass being afraid of clowns is low anyway, what with this being a clown school for so long.

I keep looking, casting the occasional glance at the teddy bear, which has remained calm and still. Maybe I imagined that the belly was moving?

Something gurgles, and I jump.

What did Hope say about this place? That it was struck by a tornado?

I shoot a look at the ceiling, which is droopy on one edge, and there's definitely light shining above, though I can't see the sky. I grab the chair at the desk and push it over to the droopy corner, but I'm still not tall enough to reach.

I'm trapped.

Trapped.

"Think, Olivia," I whisper to myself. I take two calming breaths and look around the room again.

The desk! Maybe the desk has something.

I cross the room and pull open the squeaky top drawer in the desk by the interior window just as an ominous skittering sound crackles above me.

There's something up there…

In the ceiling…

It *click-crack-clicks* its way across the drop-tiles over my head, making my skin crawl. And then the clown teddy bear shuffles in response, and something twitches in its belly again, and I scream and cringe into the corner by the desk. Because now there are two eyes glowing at me from the ceiling and noises coming from the clown and I'm probably mere seconds away from being eaten alive by the haunted circus school creatures and I won't be able to save Princess and she's such a good hedgehog, and she doesn't deserve to be orphaned, because being orphaned is the worst.

Tears sting my eyes.

God, I miss my mom.

I miss my hedgehog.

And Sir Pendleton and Savannah and Cassie and Ruthie May and even Gordon the taxidermist, because he was always polite, despite his creepy profession, and it's not his fault that he was raised with values alternative to my own.

And Jace. I miss him very most of all.

"Please don't hurt me," I whisper to the eyes.

The animal chirps, and the eyes vanish for a beat before a pudgy gray-and-black body swings down into the room Indiana Jones-style to land in the middle of the bag of clown costumes.

I stifle a scream, my heart clawing its way out of my chest when the teddy bear clown's stomach starts shrieking in response.

Shrieking? Or maybe…mewling?

Before I can decide if the sound is terrifying or maybe a little cute, the animal in the costume bag pops up, and—

"*George!* Oh my god, I'm so glad to see you!"

He chitters at me, then slinks behind the teddy clown, where an entire animal conversation goes down in between belly gurgles and twitches. Apparently, whatever is living in there and George are friends, which would be comforting if I didn't know that George has a wild side that doesn't always make the best decisions.

I could see him making friends with a rat colony, for example. If the rats had sweets and interesting trash to share.

"George, I need help," I whisper, inching closer to the stuffy. "Can you go for help? And please, *please* tell whatever's in there that we can live in harmony until someone opens the door?"

He clacks and sticks his nose out from behind the clown. A tiny gray thing follows him, followed by a larger gray thing that eyeballs me suspiciously before picking up the kitten in its mouth and slinking back into the bear's tummy.

"Kittens!" I laugh, pressing a relieved hand to my chest. "George, they're *kittens*."

He gives me a *duh, lady* look, and I hear that soothing British voice in my head again. *Raccoons can't climb sheer walls either, dear Olivia. Ask him how to get out.*

By this point I'm too freaked out to question where the voice is coming from. All I care is that it's trying to be helpful, so I beg, "George! George, can you show me how you get out of here?"

He waddles across the room and scratches at the door.

"But it's locked!"

He scratches again, then plops back on his hindquarters, clearly confused.

"So it's not locked all the time," I whisper. "George. *Now we're both trapped.*"

I wipe my brow and sneeze. There's no ventilation in here, and it's hot and sticky and I'm starting to feel queasy. But I can't let that stop me.

I have to get out. For George. For Princess. For Jace. For the kittens. Hope is going to want to rescue the heck out of those kittens, and I'm going to be the one to help her do it.

George grumbles as he shuffles over to the desk and pulls out the bottom drawer, which is completely empty, hops in, and curls up like he's going to sleep.

"No, George! We can't go to sleep. We have to find a way out. *Think*, Olivia. *Think think think.*"

I cross back to the desk and start going through the drawers again.

The top one is full of papers so old and smudged, I can't read anything that was written on them—definitely no help there. The middle drawer is more of the same—files labeled with names like *Gus, Happy, Squeezy,* and *Flowerpants.*

Clown names, the clowns who must've graduated from this school.

I lift George out of the bottom drawer, just to check that it's really empty, to find a single metal flask.

"It's so sad George," I whisper.

He chirps in seeming agreement as he crawls back into the drawer, something shiny in his hand that he uses to pick at what looks like popcorn stuck in his teeth.

No, it's not *shiny*, exactly. Just *metal*.

Like—"George! Is that a key?"

Hope flutters behind my ribs, but a moment later my shoulders sag—what good is a key when there's a chair shoved under the door handle? Still, I retrieve it from George—not wanting him to accidentally swallow it—while he waddles over to sniff another kitten, who's popped out to explore the world outside the clown bear tummy.

Maybe I can use the key to pry the window out? When I straighten, my heart leaps.

There's a small lock on one side of the window! "George! We might be getting out! Good boy!"

Not nearly as excited as he should be by this news, he disappears behind the teddy bear and emerges on the other side. As he dives back into the costume bag, I turn to the window and shimmy the key into the lock.

It's old and rusty, but the key finally goes in. It takes even more shimmying to get it to turn, and my hands are slick with sweat and I have to pause three times to sneeze, but finally the lock turns, and a soft breeze flows through the window.

I push, and it swings open wide. It's narrow—maybe not quite big enough for me to get my shoulders through—but it's open.

"George," I whisper again. "George, can you pull the chair out from under the door and unlock it?"

He chitters like that's funny, which it probably is—because he's a raccoon, not a human in a raccoon costume who can understand me.

Except he knows popcorn. His vocabulary is at least one human word long.

"George! George, if you can get the door open, I'll give you popcorn every day for the rest of my life! Which will hopefully be longer than a day or two, but I won't know if I don't get out."

He pops his head up from the bag with a shoe hooked over his face so I can't see his eyes. He shakes once, twice, and the shoe falls off, but he doesn't move to help me.

That's it, then—I'm going to have to try to climb out the window and hope I don't get stuck.

"You can do this," I whisper to myself. "Think narrow thoughts."

It's tight.

Really tight.

And I'm going to be wiggling out headfirst, which means I could end up falling on my head, and I don't know what's in that bag of trash under the window—could be a bag of dirty needles a squatter left here after shooting up under the clown mural—but I have to get out. So I stand on the desk and I reach my arms through, wedging my shoulders past the tight spot until I get caught on my hips. And then I wiggle and twist until finally—*finally*—I drop to the floor with a shriek, landing on the dusty plastic bag full of relatively soft trash. It cushions my fall, while also making me sneeze again until my eyes are watering.

I'm free.

Free.

Sort of.

I still have to get out of the building. "Thank you,

George!" I call. "Use the window, friend. I'll be back with help for you and the kittens!"

And then I take off as fast as I can through the building, looking for an exit.

"I'm coming for you, Princess," I whisper.

And Jace.

TWENTY-SEVEN

Jace

The *clown school*?

"You have got to be fucking kidding me," Blake mutters.

I ditched my truck at the edge of town — worried Ginger had spotted me following her in her rearview mirror — but Blake was only a few blocks away. I called and had him pick up her tail, then jogged over here to meet him at her final destination.

Now, we're watching her jiggle a key in the door of the closest building, a metal-sided monstrosity that I went into once as a kid for a gymnastics class before I informed my parents that I was never getting within a mile of a clown — or even a painting of a clown — ever again.

Place creeped me the fuck out.

And I'm not the only one. It's a recurring conversation in the bar.

They planning to do anything with that old circus place? someone will ask.

Hush, someone else inevitably responds. *The first rule of having a haunted clown school in your town is not talking about the haunted clown school.*

And then there will be arguing about whether or not the school can be haunted if no clowns actually died there—can clowns that died somewhere else return to haunt the place that encouraged them to become something fucked up like a clown in the first place?—until the conversation finally dissolves into laughter or shouting, depending on the intoxication levels of the pondering fools in question.

"What the hell is she doing here?" Blake mumbles with a shake of his head.

"It makes sense, though," I mutter back. "And it's proof Chester's in on it. Didn't he inherit this mess from his mom when she ditched town?"

He stiffens beside me as his whip-fast brain follows that bit of info to its logical conclusion. "Fuck, Jace. You can't be here."

"I'm following my jilted fiancée. I can be wherever the hell she is."

Ginger gets the door unlocked. She pulls it open, but before she can enter, a whirlwind with long blond hair streaming out from behind her explodes out the front door.

"You!" Ginger shrieks.

Olivia.

Olivia!

I take off at a run while Olivia spins, gaping wide-eyed at Ginger. "Princess! What did you do with Princess?"

"Chucked her body in the trash, where I'm going to chuck yours!"

I can *feel* fear take root in Olivia, but I'm close, and I won't let anyone hurt her. Hopefully she can feel that too. I sprint faster with Blake right on my heels, the two of us quickly closing the distance to the two women, but we're not fast enough.

Before we reach them, Ginger lunges for Olivia, who leaps out of the way, spins, and darts across the grounds away from us.

Ginger lifts the skirts on her wedding dress and takes off too.

We're surrounded by buildings with peeling blue and red and yellow paint, half-destroyed by a tornado that barely missed the entire town fifteen years ago. There's a ravaged clown face laughing at us on the side of one building as we run, and I swear it's laughing at *me*, taunting me that I'm going to be too late to save the woman I love.

"Stop!" I call out, but neither of the women seems to hear me. Probably because Olivia is screaming, "Help! Please! *Help me!*" while Ginger screeches, "I'm going to catch you, you homewrecking bitch! And when I do I'm going to wring your scrawny neck!"

"Citizen's arrest!" Blake shouts. "Leave her alone, Ginger! Or you're going to be even more fucked than you are already."

Olivia glances over her shoulder at the sound of Blake's voice. Our eyes connect, and she stumbles. Blake and I are closing in on them, but her pause gives Ginger enough time to leap onto her back with a wild cry.

My heart makes the leap with her, jolting straight out of my chest.

What if she has a knife?

Or a gun.

Or a rock.

Or—*fuck*. "Ginger! The baby! Think about the baby!" I yell.

"She's not pregnant!" Olivia cries out, batting at

Ginger's hands as she spins in a wincing circle, wearing a crazed redhead like a backpack.

Time slows as her words hit.

Penetrate.

Explode through the back of my skull.

Not pregnant. Ginger's not pregnant?

"She's faking it," Olivia shouts. "She was never having a baby, it was all a trick. She's seeing a fertility specialist. And changing cat litter. And lying to you!"

Ginger grabs her by the hair and yanks her head back, sending anger rushing through me. "Shut up, you whore. You don't know what you're talking about."

"Let her *go*, Ginger." My pulse ringing in my ears, I sprint the last few feet and grab Ginger around her wrists before she can pull Olivia's hair again. "Stop it," I hiss. "Stop *right now*."

"Jace, she's trying to hurt me," Ginger says, turning on the waterworks like she's a faucet, while clinging to Olivia with her legs like the world's biggest baby howler monkey. "She locked me in the clown college—"

"Enough with the lies, Ginger. Let—*oof*—go." I try to pull her off Olivia and take an elbow to the gut in the process. Blake steps in, wrapping an arm around Ginger's waist, but she has a grip of steel and there's a hatred burning in her eyes that I've never seen before, and fuck.

Fuck.

There's blood smeared on Olivia's thigh beneath her little crocheted dress.

She's bleeding.

She's fucking bleeding.

"I'll pull out every hair on her stupid lying head," Ginger screeches.

"Stop, please," Olivia begs. Tears are leaking from behind her closed eyes, and it's breaking my heart. I want to hold her, take her away from this insanity, get her the medical attention she needs, and promise her I'll never be a dumbass again.

But I can't do anything to make this better until I get Ginger off of her. "This won't end well any way you cut it, Ginger," I say. "Let her go."

"We can get you help," Olivia cries, wincing in pain.

"Jesus, Ginger, think of the baby," I say desperately. "If you're really pregnant, like you say you are, then you're putting the baby in danger."

Finally, her grip relaxes enough that I'm able to pluck her off of Olivia and hand her over to Blake. The moment Ginger's removed, Olivia sinks to her knees, clutching her stomach.

I drop down beside her, wrapping an arm around her shoulders. "You're safe now," I whisper. "Are you hurt? Where does it hurt? You're bleeding, Liv. Where does it hurt?"

"My—hot—so—tired—my stomach—" she whispers.

"Well, well, well, what have we here?" an annoyingly familiar voice, one that makes my ass clench, drawls from behind us. "*Two* O'Dell boys assaulting women? Gentlemen, you're both under arrest."

I turn to see Chester grinning gleefully as he approaches us, two sets of handcuffs swinging from his fingers.

"And her!" Ginger yelps. "Olivia attacked me, Chester! She's going to make me lose my baby!"

"There isn't a baby." Olivia grips my hand and looks up at me, her face so pale I can see the vein in her forehead. "I don't have ironclad proof, she's right. But, Jace, I *know* she's faking it. I know it with every single cell in my body."

I look up at Ginger.

She's also pale, but her eyes are bright with rage.

"Jacey, don't listen to her," Ginger says, her voice

breathy and half an octave too high. "Women don't show until they're four or even five months along. Especially with first pregnancies."

"Take a test," Olivia says. "Right now. I'll go into the women's room at the drugstore with you."

Ginger blanches another two shades, but I don't have any more time to waste trying to figure out what the hell is going on with her. Whether Ginger is pregnant or not, she appears to be in perfect health—at least physically. Olivia, on the other hand, is bleeding and starting to tremble against me.

"I'm taking Liv to the hospital," I say to Blake. "We'll figure the rest of this out later."

"You're not going anywhere, but down on the ground," Chester orders. "You and your brother. It's not every day I get to cuff you twice, you rat-faced asshole. I'm gonna enjoy the shit out of this."

I ignore him, both because I feel like I've been run over by a spiked boulder that keeps coming back for more, and also because Olivia's moaning as I help her to her feet.

"No, Jace." Ginger grabs onto my arm, clinging tight. "Stay. We can work this out, I know we can."

"We're done," I say. "Let me go."

"You know better than to leave me, Jace O'Dell," she hisses. "You're never going to find anyone half as good as me. Certainly not that skinny bitch."

"Jesus, shut up, Ginger," Blake says. "Have you completely lost it?" He's pale too, his eyes wide, but I can't worry about my brother right now either.

Not with Olivia's body radiating heat and her breath going shallow and more blood trickling down her pale legs.

"I said get on your stomachs!" Chester barks.

I shoulder past him. "Shove it, Chester. Olivia needs medical attention."

"I need medical attention!" Ginger shrieks. "She attacked me!"

"Stop right there, Jace," Chester shouts. "All three of you are under arrest."

"You're gonna lose your badge," Blake growls. "For what? For *Ginger*? Is she worth it, Chester?"

"I'm the law around here," he snaps. "*I* say who gets locked up. And *I* say I've had enough of your whole fucking family. You're *all* going down. Even that firefighter asshole. Especially that firefighter asshole for what he did in front of my boss."

That firefighter asshole is running toward us now too, with Cassie and Hope and Sheriff Briggs...

And—what the *fuck*?

Chewpaca the alpaca is trotting along on a leash behind them, giving a mighty *moo* that makes Chester jump.

"Good Chewpaca," Hope says. "I knew you'd find her! Good nose, boy."

The alpaca strains on his lead, lunging for Olivia.

I hug her tighter. "Not right now, buddy," I tell the alpaca. "I know you love Liv, we all do, but we need to get her to the hospital."

Ginger is jerking in Blake's grip as he holds tight to her elbows, keeping her from hurting anyone else. "Sheriff!" she screams. "Sheriff, they're trying to rape me and hurt my baby!"

"You're not having a baby, Ginger," Blake snaps. "Give it up already."

"*Lies!*"

"Liv?" I say as she sags against me. "Liv? Olivia?"

But she doesn't answer, and a beat later her knees buckle.

"What in the sam hill is going on here?" the sheriff demands, but I ignore him, swooping Olivia in my arms.

Desperation claws at me.

She's hot. *So* hot. And her head is lolling back and her breath isn't right. "Ryan. *Ryan.* Help."

He shoves Chester out of the way and rushes toward me, calling over his shoulder, "Cassie, call 9-1-1. You know the routine."

"She's burning up," I tell him.

"Heat exhaustion." He points to a nearby patch of trees. "Shade. Now."

Shade. Yes. Shade.

And love.

Olivia would say love can cure anything.

"I love you, Liv," I whisper as I race her to the trees. "Hold on, Sunshine. Just hold on for me. You're gonna be okay. I promise."

Please. Please be okay.

She has to be.

She just has to be.

TWENTY-EIGHT

Jace

I hate hospitals. They smell like delays and paperwork and sickness all masked beneath a sickly evergreen antiseptic spray that reeks like gin gone bad. The chairs in the waiting room are ice molded into the most uncomfortable sitting positions known to man, and the staff shoots you judgmental looks because they've seen you one too many times for stupid injuries incurred while you were being a dumb kid or a drunk idiot.

And—this evening—as a special treat, there's a sheriff's deputy guarding the entrance so I don't try to *skip town* before they sort out what went on this afternoon.

This afternoon?

It seems impossible, but it was only ten short hours ago that I woke up in Olivia's she shed thinking today was the start of the rest of my life. Now she's being treated in the emergency room for god only knows what, and they won't let me see her.

But at least George is here to keep our minds off our troubles.

Fucking *George*.

Sitting there next to Ryan eating popcorn from the vending machine and wearing a clown hat on his head.

"George led Hope to some kittens inside the building," Ryan says as he scans his phone. "He's a hero. Mama cat's too skinny and probably isn't producing enough milk so they got to those babies just in time."

I level a glare at him. "That's great. *But how the fuck is Olivia?*"

"Like I said before, she came to in the ambulance. And they're getting fluids in her. She'll be okay. And she told the paramedics George saved her too. Helped her find a way out."

I shove to my feet and pace. "I love her," I tell him.

"We know."

I jab a finger at his chest. "You wanted me to marry someone else yesterday."

He sighs and shoves his hands through his hair. "Jace, I didn't *want* you to. But I knew you'd be an amazing father, and you needed legal protection to make sure she couldn't keep the baby from you."

"You think Ginger is really faking the pregnancy?" I ask. The words are hard to utter. I don't know if Olivia's right, but if she is, I'm both relieved and disappointed at the same time.

All my hopes and dreams for the kid—taking him or her to baseball, ballet, or soccer, catching them sneaking out because I know every last trick in the book, and I wouldn't let my kid repeat my mistakes, birthdays with presents and cakes—they're all evaporating.

Because it makes sense.

Ginger is supposed to be more than three months along, and her stomach's still as flat as it was in Mexico. No morning sickness. No cravings. Add in all the attempts to seduce me, and the fact that, in the midst of all of this afternoon's drama, she didn't once ask to see a doctor, and I smell a rat.

A redheaded, not-at-all pregnant one.

"You ever see a positive test?" Ryan asks.

I shake my head. "No. I just trusted her."

He makes a sound that I know is his *dumbass, always ask to see a pregnancy test* noise, even though none of us have ever needed to think about that before.

"I wanted to do the right thing," I say defensively.

He rises and claps me on the shoulder. "You *did* do the right thing. You know how proud of you we all are? Your teenage years were hell, but you got your life back on track. Now you run your own business, you have your own home, and you stepped up to the plate to take responsibility when your partner said she was pregnant. You *are* one of the good guys, Jace, whether you like it or not. So suck it up and own it."

His phone vibrates again, and we both look down.

"Aw, look. Princess got a swimming pool." He angles the phone so I can see the picture Cassie sent of Princess von Spooksalot sniffing at the wide, shallow water bowl in a cage in Hope's office.

"Does Olivia know she's okay?" I ask.

He nods.

I didn't get to ride with her in the ambulance because *family only, Mr. O'Dell.* Ryan managed to sneak in under the guise of being her first responder.

"Mr. O'Dell?"

"Yes?" Ryan and I both spin and answer together.

I elbow him in the gut, and he gives me a sheepish grin. "Habit. Sorry. Go ahead."

The nurse nods to me. "Ms. Moonbeam is asking to see you."

I hurry to follow her, stepping on the back of her shoes more than once while she guides me through the winding passageway to the room where Olivia's resting on a bed. "Sorry," I mutter. "Drinks on me next time you're in the Wild Hedgehog. Hog. Wild Hog."

She pulls the curtain closed around us. I rush to Olivia's side.

"Hey. How are you?" I brush her hair out of her pale face, and she smiles at me. "Feeling better?"

"Much better." She beams up at me. "Thank you. For saving me."

I choke on a laugh, because she's still so pale, and has dark circles under her eyes, and is hooked up to an IV and wearing a hospital gown that makes her look ridiculously frail and I'm so fucking worried for her my heart is about to wring itself out. "You saved yourself, Sunshine."

"With help from my friends."

I squeeze her hand, stroke her hair, kiss her forehead once, twice because it's impossible to keep my hands off of her. I'm just so glad she's okay. "I'm so sorry, Liv. I shouldn't have left you alone this morning."

"It was meant to—to—tooooo-*choo*!" She shakes her head, then smiles sweetly at me. "To be," she finishes with a whisper. "A necessary evil."

I shake my head. "No. It's never necessary for you to be hurt. *Ever*."

She lifts a breezy shoulder. "It always hurts to grow. Sometimes a little, sometimes a lot, but we come out on the other side, and we're better for it."

I bend and kiss her again. "You're a saint, woman."

"But you're okay, right? Like Ryan said?" she whispers while she strokes my cheek. "I didn't know if they'd hurt you, too."

I shake my head. "No. They didn't hurt me. Other than by hurting you, I mean."

The curtain pulls back, and another nurse sticks her head in. "Ms. Moonbeam? We need to get your temperature one more time."

She looks pointedly at me, but Liv grips my hand hard. "He can stay. He's family."

Family. I don't know what I did to deserve her, but my heart is swelling with gratitude and love and happiness.

"I love you," I tell her huskily.

"I love you—oo—oooo-*choo*!"

"And you have the cutest sneezes."

"They're starting to annoy me." She twitches her nose and opens wide for the thermometer.

"Dry sinuses are a perfectly normal symptom, and often lead to sneezing. Though I would say you've got an extreme case," the nurse says. "The doctor can prescribe a nasal irrigator, and plenty of fluids should help. Of course, you'll need the extra fluids anyway until the baby comes."

Olivia chokes on the thermometer.

I swivel my head to stare at the nurse. "What does Ginger faking a pregnancy have to do with Olivia sneezing and needing fluids?"

I get new-age mumbo-jumbo happens, but not in a hospital.

And Ginger *was* faking it.

Wasn't she?

Fuck. I can't make her pee on a stick. And even if I did, there are health privacy laws in place that mean she wouldn't have to show me the results.

The nurse stares back at me blankly, like I'm a crazy person, because, let's be honest here, that wasn't a normal question. But it hasn't been a normal day, not for me or Olivia.

"Baby?" Olivia asks.

Now the nurse's eyes go wide. "Oh, no," she mutters. "They didn't tell you?"

"Who…wha—aaa*choo*?"

Without another word, the nurse ducks back out of the curtain.

"Jace?" Olivia whispers. "What's she talking about?"

I settle onto the bed next to her and pull her close, being careful to not disturb her IV, my heart moving into an entirely different space. A hopeful, maybe-miracles-do-come-true space.

We both stare at the curtain.

"I love you," I say again, because it's the truest thing I've ever said and I know I'm never going to get tired of telling her. And because maybe…

Just maybe…

She squeezes my thigh. "I love you too."

The curtain swishes, and a middle-aged doctor that I think once set my arm after a fall from a barn roof steps into the room. "Ms. Moonbeam. The nurse tells me you—ah. Sir, if you could just step outside a moment?"

"No," Olivia and I say together. She smiles at me. "He stays. He's family."

"You're my everything," I say, soft but sure.

"You're certain about that?" The doctor looks between us as though he knows that twenty-four hours ago, I was running away from marrying the mother of my child who's not actually carrying my child.

Fuck, my life is crazy.

"I want him here. No matter what you have to say," Olivia tells him.

He nods. "Okay. The nurse tells me no one told you the results of your pelvic exam. For the bleeding. I apologize for that. We're short staffed, too many people out with the summer flu."

She frowns and leans into me.

My heart's in my throat, because *baby* and *bleeding* don't go together. Even I know that.

"But everything's fine," he assures her. "And spotting is normal in early pregnancy. We'll just want to—"

"Pregnancy?" she whispers. "I'm pregnant? Me?"

"Blood test just confirmed it," he says, his tired eyes blinking. "I'm sorry, I didn't realize that you—"

"Pregnancy?" I repeat, wanting to be one hundred percent sure I'm hearing him right.

He shifts uncomfortably. "Ms. Moonbeam, if you'd prefer to discuss this in private—"

"No. He stays." She sneezes twice, then peers up at him again. "Tell us everything please."

The doc hesitates another moment before he sighs and says, "Well, judging by the hormone levels, you're about six weeks along. Though we'd like to do an ultrasound before you're discharged, to check baby's heartbeat before you go, just to be on the safe side."

Six weeks.

Six weeks.

"It happened the night at the bar," she says, meeting my gaze. "We must have messed up with the condom because I haven't— And *I hadn't*, not in a long time— And well you're — We're—"

"Yeah." My eyes are getting hot, and it's suddenly almost impossible to swallow. "We are," I breathe.

"We're having a baby. A human baby." A grin curves her pretty mouth, and her sunshine smile lights up the entire room, the way it always does, making me start laughing like a damned fool.

A happy fool.

The happiest fool in the world.

"Well, it's unlikely to be a raccoon," the doctor replies with a smile. "So it seems like this is good news."

"Yes!" Olivia exclaims. Her lashes flutter and she turns to me. "Right? I mean…it is. Isn't it? That's why you're laughing?" She giggles, clinging tighter to my hand.

I can't talk, so I nod. A lot.

And then I pull her in tight and I kiss her, because *this*.

This — Olivia? Having my baby? Having *our* baby?

Nothing has ever been so right.

"So happy," I finally manage to say.

"Me too!" She sneezes, and then she laughs. "We're having a baby. I can't wait to tell Princess and Sir Pendleton. They'll be delighted."

"I love you," I tell her again.

"Oh! And your parents. And Cassie and Ryan and Blake. And Hope! I have to tell Hope." She frowns. "But should we wait? I mean, until we're sure everything's one hundred percent…okay?"

"Pretty sure everything's fine," the doc assures her. "But we'll have you taken up to ultrasound as soon as they can get a wheelchair down here. Let you two see the flashing light."

Thirty minutes later, we're watching a tiny light flash on a small screen in a dark room, while Olivia grips my hands and I grip hers right back.

It's our baby's heartbeat.

We're going to have a baby.

I feel like the luckiest man in the world.

"I'm going to do right by you, Liv," I whisper.

"You already have," she whispers back. "All I need is you."

"You have me, Sunshine. All of me. Forever."

EPILOGUE

Olivia

Having a wedding feels unnecessary—Jace has been my husband in my heart since the night we made love in the Wild Hog.

But I love celebrations and happiness and *family*, and that's exactly what we're celebrating today in the O'Dells' backyard.

"Isn't it exciting, Princess?" My sweet little girl—dressed in a tiny bridesmaid outfit and chilling in a basket full of flower petals resting on the narrow table next to me —purrs softly, proving she's thrilled to be a part of the celebration.

Now that her evil ex, the abusive hedgie stud known as Quillie Nelson, has been shipped off to a rehabilitation facility—and Chester has lost his breeder's license for abandoning Princess in the park—she's thriving.

And hardly humping at all anymore. At least not

humping Sir P, though she has been pretty into her new stuffed raccoon toy.

"I'm so glad you're here," I murmur, stroking her quills below her flower crown. "You've been there since the beginning of Daddy and me. And you're family too."

"Well, of course she is." Cassie hurries up the porch steps and into the hallway beside me, the flower-festooned yard and the gemstone-covered reception tables behind her looking like something out of a fairy tale—the one where the princess wakes up and realizes her real-life prince is even better than in her dreams.

I can't wait to see Jace, to kiss him and promise him forever, and mean it with every beat of my heart.

"Almost ready?" Cassie asks, eyeing my forehead before she shouts over my shoulder, "Van, we need you! Flower emergency! Crowns are crooked!"

I laugh. "I'm sure it's not an emergency. Jace will still love me if my crown is crooked."

She beams up at me, her eyes shining. "Of course he will. Oh my god, I'm going to cry through this entire ceremony aren't I?"

"If you do, they'll be happy tears," Savannah says, bustling in from the kitchen where she's been putting the finishing touches on a cake so beautiful I almost hate to eat it.

But I will, because I love cake almost as much as I love these two amazing sister-friends.

"I'm so glad you're home for a visit," I say, hugging Savannah again, even though I've already squeezed her sweet self at least a dozen times since her plane touched down yesterday.

She returns the embrace. "Me too! Now lean down for the height challenged, gorgeous," she says, lifting her arms to gently shift and re-pin my crown of rosemary for remembrance for my mom, lavender for devotion and harmony in my marriage, and the loveliest purple roses for love at first sight.

For Jace and me it was love at first aura-brush, but sight is close enough.

"There. Perfect." Savannah blinks up at me, a flicker of sadness threading through her energy again, the same one I noticed last night while we were having tea and girl talk that I can't seem to hug away. "I'm so happy for you, Livvy." She takes my hands, giving them both a firm squeeze. "*So* happy. Jace is clearly all in with this and I adore how protective he is of you."

"He's worse than Ryan," Cassie says with a smile. "Drives her to work every morning so she and Princess can both sit in the sidecar and watch the world go by."

"He's very attentive," I say with a blush. *Attentive* isn't a strong enough word for how thoroughly he loved me this morning before finally letting me leave our bed to go for a pedicure with my besties before the wedding.

"Well, you can't really blame him, what with Ginger and Chester out there on the streets, threatening the safety and decency of Happy Cat at large," Cassie says, opening an arm as Hope slips into the hall from the porch and pulling her in for a side hug.

"What are we talking about?" Hope asks, a little out of breath. But she's officiating the wedding—and in charge of getting Chewpaca dressed for his trot down the aisle as best man—and has been busy with all the last minute preparations.

She still looks lovely in her sunflower print dress, however, and remarkably fresh considering it's almost ninety degrees again today. August in Georgia isn't ideal wedding weather, but it would take a lot more than heat and humidity to curdle my spirits.

"Talking about the stupid judge who let Ginger and Chester out on bail before their trials," Cassie says with a sniff.

Hope's brows lift. "Oh. Right. But I don't think either of them will try anything again. They can't, really. If they so much as sneeze the wrong way, Ruthie May will post it on InstaChat before they have time to get a tissue."

Savannah hugs me again. "Ugh. I still can't believe that sociopath locked you in the clown school. I mean, I always knew she wasn't quite right, but geez..."

She shudders, and my heart does a little leap at the memory of being held captive, but soon settles back into a normal rhythm. Because Hope's right—neither Ginger nor Chester are threats anymore.

Ginger will always be a manipulative schemer, but the day she posted bail, Jace met her for coffee, they had a long heart-to-heart, and came to an understanding that put his mind at ease.

I didn't ask what the understanding was, but considering she's lost her job, all her credibility, and Chester confessed to donating sperm to help her get pregnant so she could trick Jace into marrying her, further smearing her good name, I trust that she's learned the error of her ways. And if either she or Chester violate the restraining orders Jace filed against them, they'll go right back to jail.

I feel safe again in Happy Cat, the way I always have, the way I hope my family will for years and years to come.

"I really love Ruthie May," Hope adds with a sigh. "But I'd love her even more if she'd quit speculating on my love life in public."

"But she's a good-hearted busybody," Cassie says. "And since Savannah offered her the CEO role at Sunshine Toys yesterday, pretty soon she's going to be too busy with work to keep up with anything but the juiciest, most important gossip."

"Lovely! I look forward to fading back into obscurity by summer's end." Hope picks a piece of lint off my dress, a stunning vintage lace number my mom picked out when she was pregnant with me, before she realized a wedding wasn't in her story.

Her spirit is always with me, but I'm even closer to her today. I know she's so happy for me. And Jace. And this precious little one who's going to join our family next spring.

"Hey girls!" Mrs. O'Dell calls out, waving from the bottom of the porch steps, her green eyes sparkling and her pink cheeks even pinker today, with excitement. "The groom is ready whenever the bride is." She blows a kiss my way. "You're beautiful, sweetheart. So happy you're joining our family!'

"Me too! We'll be right out, Minnie!" I wave back and then bring a hand to rest on my belly. It's still too early for me to be showing, but I can feel my son or daughter in there, safe and loved and growing stronger every day. "We're getting married, baby," I whisper. "And you're going to have the best daddy ever. You're going to love him. I promise."

Savannah blinks quickly, while Cassie sniffles and swipes at the tears rolling down her cheeks. "See! I'm crying. And we haven't even started yet!"

Hope beams at all three of us. "Y'all are the sweetest and the best and I'm so happy to be a part of this day. Come on. Let's go get this adorable couple hitched."

We file out of the house and down the porch steps with Hope in the lead. She stops beneath the shade tree at the edge of the yard to collect Chewpaca's leash—and to keep our best man from eating the flowers from my crown as he moos his congratulations into the breezy air. Then my lovely bridesmaids hook arms with their groomsmen, Blake takes Princess's basket tenderly in hand, and we head for the creek.

And there, just shy of the bridge that stretches over the swimming hole, my man is waiting.

For me.

Even in just a simple white button-down linen shirt and khaki linen pants—the weather is too hot for anything more formal—he's the most beautiful thing I've ever seen

The miracle of it all makes my smile stretch even wider, until my jaw starts to hurt.

But it's a good hurt, the kind that makes you realize you're fully, incredibly, magnificently alive.

A breeze rustles the leaves on the old live oaks and the sun beams from behind fluffy summer clouds, Nature herself giving her blessing as Hope leads a proud and prancing Chewpaca down the aisle, before tying his lead to the bridge behind the small platform where she'll stand to officiate. The rest of the people we love very most of all file between the chairs set up in the shade, while more dear friends and neighbors turn to watch. First Ryan and Cassie, with George Cooney in a tuxedo bow tie waddling between them, then Blake with Princess, and finally, it's our turn.

Savannah turns to me, holding out her arm, "Ready to marry your other best friend?" she asks.

"Ready, my very first best friend," I say, my eyes stinging a little as I curl my fingers into her elbow. Visions of all the years I've shared with this lovely person—from the time when we were little girls drawing in our dream journals with glitter pens, to visits during our teen years, when we'd sneak away to the beach by my house to wish out loud for magical, fearless grown-up lives, to our move to Happy Cat to start a bold and love-focused business together—flicker on my mental screen, making me so grateful.

For the love I've had.

And for the love waiting in my future.

Heart overflowing and aura burning bright, I start down the aisle with her. Jace's eyes meet mine and hold and suddenly there's no one else under the trees.

No one else in the world. No one but him, this person who isn't perfect, but who is absolutely perfect for me.

As Savannah drops me at the end of the aisle, I transfer my bouquet to my left hand and reach for Jace with my right. He takes my palm, cradling it between both of his with a tenderness that is all I need to feel that an unbreakable promise has been made.

His eyes shine, and a smile touches his lips as he whispers, "I thought you'd come down the aisle on your Vespa."

I grin as I whisper back, "You looking for a getaway car, buddy?"

"Never," he says, his smile falling away. "I only want to get closer to you, Sunshine. Today and every day."

Hope, the only one who can hear us, sighs happily and asks in a soft voice, "You lovebirds ready?"

"Ready," we both say at the same time, laughing as Hope raises her voice to begin.

"Dearly beloved folks of Happy Cat, we gather today to celebrate the love of two beautiful people…." Her voice lilts up and down and Jace and I speak our parts in turn— promising to love and cherish, to honor and protect—but it's the words that aren't spoken that mean the most. It's the look in his eyes, the one that promises he's never going to let me go. It's the awe in his voice, leaving no doubt that what we have is as precious to him as it is to me. It's the magic in his kiss, as he pulls me into his arms to seal the deal, that makes my heart soar up into the sky to explode in a million glittery bits of stardust that rain down on the world, making it better than it was before.

"Love makes it all better," I whisper against his lips.

"Amen," he whispers back.

"And also cake," I murmur as Jace pulls back and the sounds of our friends and families' applause fill the air.

He grins. "I love you."

"More than cake?" I ask, beaming back at my husband. My Kindred Penis. My all things good and right and wonderful.

"More than cake," he promises, and then he kisses me again. And again. Until Chewpaca gets loose and inserts himself between us, managing to get his tongue back in my ear before Hope recaptures his lead.

And then Princess is in my arms, purring and trembling with excitement as we head for the reception. There, George has already managed to submerge himself in the punch bowl and is wearing a pineapple ring as a bracelet on each paw while Clint, Jace's other brother, who just barely made it home as a surprise, is shrugging and helping himself to punch anyway.

"It's a Marine thing," Jace tells me with a grin.

We have champagne and seltzer for the rest of us, so no one's too upset.

And then there is dancing and more dancing and a mini-fireworks show put on by the firehouse boys as the sun goes down. And then Jace and I are climbing onto my Vespa to head for home with our hedgehog baby asleep in her basket and our human baby safe inside her mama and the dusky sky full of shooting stars.

But I don't wish on any of them.

I leave those wishes for other people.

All of mine have already come true.

SNEAK PEEK AT MAGNIFICENT BASTARD

Love sexy, flirty, dirty romantic comedy? Then you're going to love the USA Today Bestseller, Magnificent Bastard by Lili Valente! Keep reading for a sneak peek...

ABOUT THE BOOK

MAGNIFICENT BASTARD

F*CK **Prince Charming. Sometimes, you need a Magnificent Bastard.**

FACE IT, ladies: love sucks and then you cry...while your ex rides off into the sunset banging your best friend.

BUT WHY LET a break-up end in tears when it can end

with sweet revenge? Enter Magnificent Bastard Consulting and me, chief executive bastard. I've got it all—looks, brains, a heart of gold, and the killer instinct guaran-damn-teed to make your ex regret the day he said goodbye.

WITH THE HELP of my virtual assistant, I've built an empire giving broken-hearted women the vengeance they deserve, while keeping myself far from the front lines of the heart. Life is a bowl of cherries, until my *virtual* assistant shows up on my *real* doorstep for the first time, begging for a Magnificent Bastard intervention of her own.

DAMN... **She's a bona fide sex kitten.**

I PRIDE myself on being a true pro, but pretending to be her lover soon leads to giving it to her good, hard, fast, and up against the wall. And somewhere between getting balls deep in my sweet and sexy assistant and watching her ex beg for a second chance, I break every last one of my damn rules—professional *and* personal.

SO WHAT'S my next move? Fight for the girl who makes me want to get up on a white horse and ride to her rescue, or stay a Magnificent Bastard to the end?

WARNING: **MAGNIFICENT BASTARD is a stand-alone erotic romance told from the hero's point of view. No cliffhanger. Lots of dirty talk.**

• • •

EXCERPT

PICTURE THIS: it's a rainy spring day in the city. The streets are covered with a fine layer of mud and soggy garbage, the sun is a distant memory from another, brighter time when you were still stupid enough to believe in happy endings, and you've just been dumped so hard your heart looks like it's gone three rounds with Mike Tyson.

You're ugly crying in a corner with a box of wine and a chocolate bar the size of your forearm, wishing Prince Charming would come swoop you up on his white horse and carry you far away from all those nasty memories of Mr. Wrong, but I'm here to tell you, ladies—

You need to stop that shit.

Stop it. Right now.

Why? Because Prince Charming is a crock of shit. Like unicorns, mermen, and other fairy tale creatures, he doesn't exist.

When you're down and out and your heart has been ripped to shreds by an asshole with a dickish-side a mile wide, you don't need Prince Charming. You need a man who's not afraid to get his hands dirty, a man who can teach Mr. Wrong a thing or two about what it feels like to be deceived, betrayed, and laid low by the one person in the world you thought you could trust. What you need is a Magnificent Bastard, your very own one-man vengeance machine.

Love isn't a fairy tale, sweetheart; it's war, and now you've got a soldier with an anti-asshole missile on your side.

Want to ruin your ex's reputation? No problem. Every true asshole has a few skeletons in his closet and I specialize in spring cleaning. Want to send that human come stain to jail? A little harder, but often still possible. I only accept cases involving the very worst examples of mankind, the most miserable liars, cheats, and scoundrels. Truly terrible people tend to be good at covering their tracks, but I've delivered exes in cuffs before.

Want to make your former lover green with envy? Make him wish he'd never kicked you off the love wagon, spat in your face, and walked away? Well, that, cupcake…

That's what I'm best at.

I've been blessed with a face that turns heads, worked hard for a body that inspires shudders of lust at twenty paces, and honed my envy-inspiring skills into a razor sharp weapon I wield with ruthless efficiency. I will make you feel like a queen and ensure your ex doesn't miss a minute of it. You'll be treated like a treasure, pampered like a princess, and kissed like a slut who can't get enough of my magnificent dick.

In reality, of course, things between us will never go further than a kiss, but your ex won't know that. He'll see your flushed cheeks, lust-glazed eyes, and wobbly legs and think I'm giving it to you hard every night.

He'll imagine my hands on your ass, my fingers slipping between your legs, and your pussy slick just for me. He'll imagine you screaming my name while you ride my cock and remember all the times he was lucky enough to be balls deep in your incomparable snatch. Before long, he'll have a jealousy hard-on so bad he'll come crawling back to you on his belly, begging for a second chance.

But you won't give it to him.

Did you hear that?

Even so, it bears repeating—

You. Will not. Give that loser a second chance.

By the time I'm through with you, you will know deep down in the marrow of your bones that you're better than that. You'll realize that you deserve a man whose eyes won't wander, whose hands won't hurt, and whose heart belongs to you and only you. You'll be able to look down at the sniveling, pathetic, limp-dicked excuse for a man you used to love and tell him that he has no power over you.

Not anymore. Now you're free to move on with your life without any of the bad breakup, psychic baggage.

And that, gorgeous, is the most important of the services I deliver. I give you back to *you*, the only person who can be trusted to steer your course as you ride off into the sunset.

But if for some reason, you break this all-important rule, if you sour the gift you've been given by going back to Major Dickweed, don't bother contacting me again. No amount of money will convince me to pick up the phone.

A Magnificent Bastard intervention is a once in a life-time opportunity. One and done, no exceptions.

None.

Not even for her, the woman who made me break all my rules, the woman who made me think—for one amazing week—that even magnificent bastards can live happily ever after.

MAGNIFICENT BASTARD IS AVAILABLE NOW!

SNEAK PEEK AT FLIRTING WITH THE FRENEMY

If you're into enemies to lovers, brother's best friend, and single dads, read on for a sample of Pippa Grant's **FLIRTING WITH THE FRENEMY!**

ELLIE RYDER, aka a woman in need of more than ice cream to fill the hole in her heart

WHEN I RULE THE WORLD, peppermint crunch ice cream will be available all year long, because assholes who break people's hearts don't restrict their assholery and heart-breaking to Christmas.

Unless, apparently, they're *my* asshole.

Check that.

My *former* asshole.

I stab my spoon straight into the cold carton that I grabbed at the store on the way here and ignore the twinkling holiday cheer on my parents' gigantic tree in the living room. It's late, so I didn't tell them I was coming over, but I don't want to spend one more night at my house this week.

Alone.

Sleeping in the bed where Patrick screwed me — and then screwed me over — just two nights ago.

Merry Christmas, Ellie. I'm in love with my neighbor.

I leave them a note taped to the coffee pot to let them know I'm here, then stomp down the stairs — softly, so I don't wake them — and turn the corner into the rec room, where I pound the light switch up.

And then almost scream.

There's a lump of a man sprawled on the couch watching a black-and-white movie, and as soon as the lights go on, he winces and throws his arm over his eyes. "*Christ*," he snarls.

My heart backpedals from the precipice where it was about to leap, then surges into a furious beat all over again. "What the fuck are you doing here?"

Wyatt Morgan drops his arm and squints at me. "Oh, good. It's Ellie. Drop in to rub some salt in the wound?"

I inhale another bite of ice cream while I glare at him, because I didn't ask *him* to be here, and he's scowling just as hard as I'm glaring. "Beck's place is downtown. Go get drunk there." Even as the words leave my mouth, guilt stabs me in the lung.

Not the heart, because first, I'd have to *like* my brother's best friend for my heart to be affected, and second, because I'm not sure I have a heart left.

I'm in a shit-tastic mood — who dumps their girlfriend *on Christmas Eve?* — but even in the midst of my own pity party, I know why Wyatt's sitting in my parents' basement, stewing himself in beer and watching *It's a Wonderful Life*.

He doesn't even roll his eyes at my order to get out.

"Beck's having a party," he informs me. "Didn't want to

go. Guess you weren't invited. Or you prefer to add to the shit pile here."

He tips back his beer, and another guilt knife attacks me, this time in the liver.

It's entirely possible he has bigger problems than I do. I lost a boyfriend that I'll probably acknowledge soon enough —for real, not just in a fit of anger—that I'm better off without.

The courts just handed Wyatt a final divorce decree that means he only gets to see his kid once a month.

If he travels five hundred miles to do it every time.

"Shove it, Morgan," I tell him. "I don't kick a man when he's down."

"Since when?"

"Oh, please. Like you can talk."

It's been like this since we were kids. My brother's childhood best friend is the only man in the entire universe who can get under my skin and bring out my ugly faster than you can blink, and I swear he takes joy in doing it.

A ninety-five on your math test, Ellie? Why not perfect?

Nice shot, but you're still down by eight.

Who taught you to hold a pool cue, a blind monkey?

And damn if all that taunting didn't make me try harder every fucking time.

Because when he wasn't taunting me, he was the first one holding out a hand to pull me off the pavement or out of the mud when I inevitably got trampled trying to keep up with Beck and his friends in soccer, street hockey, basketball, and whatever else I swore I was big enough to do with them.

He eyeballs my breasts, and my whole body lights up like the Christmas lights all over downtown.

"You gonna eat that whole carton?" he asks, and *fuck*, he's not looking at my chest.

He's looking at my ice cream, and here I am, getting turned on at the idea that he's finally noticed I'm a woman.

I have issues.

So many fucking issues.

I fling myself onto the couch next to him. "It's loser ice cream, so yeah, I am," I grumble. "Here. Have a bite, you drunk asshole."

Those gray eyes connect with mine, and *dammit*, that's straight lust pooling in my belly.

He's sporting a thick five-o'clock shadow, and even sprawled out on the worn flowery couch in my parents' basement, he exudes power and masculinity in a way I never would've expected from the skinny pipsqueak peeking out from behind his grandmother's legs on the front porch twenty-some years ago.

Or maybe it's the tight black T-shirt, with his biceps testing the limits of the cotton and detailing his trim stomach, even sitting down, and the gray sweatpants hinting at a more substantial package than I ever would've given him credit for.

Plus the knowledge that Pipsqueak Wyatt grew up to join the Air Force as some kind of badass pilot who flies untested aircraft, which takes a hell of a lot of guts, if you ask me when I'm willing to admit something like that about him.

Which is apparently tonight.

You used to like him, my subconscious reminds me, because it's forgetting its place.

I'd tell it to shut up, that I don't go for guys who don't appreciate me, except isn't that what I just spent the last two years of my life doing?

He reaches for my spoon, and our fingers brush when he takes it. A shiver ripples over my skin. I look away to watch the movie while I hold the carton for him to dig out a scoopful.

George Bailey is arguing with Mr. Potter on the TV, and I can feel the heat off Wyatt's skin penetrating my baggy Ryder Consulting sweatshirt.

I snort softly to myself.

Of course he wasn't staring at my chest. He can't even see it under this thing.

You're holding the basketball wrong, Ellie.

It went in, didn't it?

Yeah, but you could be more consistent if you worked on your form.

Damn him for sneaking into my head. Damn him for taunting me.

Damn him for being right.

Because I did work on my fucking form, and Beck—who's three years older than I am—quit playing ball with me after I beat him in a free throw contest when I was twelve.

He said it was because he was *working on other stuff with the guys*, but I knew my brother better than that.

I *knew* he quit playing with me because I beat him.

Wyatt still took the challenge though. He'd tell me I got lucky when I won. He'd tell me what I did wrong when I didn't.

And I worked my ass off getting better and better until I beat him *every time*.

And then he lost interest too.

I take the spoon from him and grunt softly while I dig deeper into the carton. "You were such an asshole when we were kids."

He grunts back and snags the spoon again. "*You* were such an asshole when we were kids."

"You were just insecure about getting your ass beat by a girl on the basketball court."

"You just hated that you wouldn't have been half as good without me."

I take my spoon back and shovel in. My extra-large bite of ice cream makes my brain cramp, but fuck if I'll let him see me hurt.

Not that I can hide it. I know my face is blotchy from crying before I drove over here, and my eyes are that special kind of dry that comes after too many tears.

I can count on one hand the number of times I've talked to him solo since he and Beck and the guys graduated high school. He's changed. His voice is deeper, if that's possible. His body definitely harder—*god*, those biceps, and his forearms are tight, with large veins snaking over the corded muscle from his elbows to his knuckles—his square jaw more chiseled, his eyes steel rather than simple gray.

And it's not like he lost custody of his kid because he's an asshole.

Beck was blabbering all about it at Christmas dinner yesterday. *Dude got so fucked. The military gave him orders here, so Lydia moved first, with Tucker. She hated military life. But then his orders got changed last-minute so he ended up in Georgia, she filed for divorce, and he's been fighting the military and the courts ever since to get back to where he can be closer to his kid. He's in fucking hell right now. And if he cuts bait on the military, they'll toss him in jail for being AWOL. He's fucked. He's SO fucked.*

There goes George Bailey, leaving Mr. Potter's office to go get drunk.

Wyatt tips back his beer. A holiday brew. Like that can take away the misery of hurting this time of year. I don't know why he's here instead of taking advantage of every last minute with his kid, but then, I don't know much about divorce either.

Maybe this isn't his Christmas to see his son. Maybe Lydia's being an asshole.

One more bottle sits on the end table next to him, but just one.

Drowning his sorrows with a broken George Bailey.

"I'm sorry about your shitty divorce," I say.

Sullenly.

Just in case he thinks I might have a twinge of sympathy for him. That won't do for either of us.

He sets the bottle down and grabs the spoon again.

"So you're sharing because you feel sorry for me."

"Maybe I'm sharing because I'm not a total asshole."

"But I still am?"

I heave a sigh. I don't want to be sitting here with Wyatt Morgan any more than I want to give in to the urge to go running over to Patrick's swanky condo in the Warehouse district and beg him to give us another chance.

I was supposed to be getting engaged this Christmas.

Not dumped.

And I can't tell if that searing pain in my chest is my heart or my pride.

Or both.

FLIRTING with the Frenemy is available now!

ABOUT THE AUTHORS

Pippa Grant is a stay-at-home mom and housewife who loves to escape into sexy, funny stories way more than she likes perpetually cleaning toothpaste out of sinks and off toilet handles. When she's not reading, writing, sleeping, or trying to prepare her adorable demon spawn to be productive members of society, she's fantasizing about chocolate chip cookies.

Find Pippa at…
www.pippagrant.com
pippa@pippagrant.com

Author of over forty novels, *USA Today* Bestseller Lili Valente writes everything from steamy suspense to laugh-out-loud romantic comedies. A die-hard romantic and optimist at heart, she can't resist a story where love wins big. Because love should always win.

When she's not writing, Lili enjoys adventuring with her two sons, climbing on rocks, swimming too far from shore, and asking "why" an incorrigible number of times per day. A former yoga teacher, actor, and dancer, she is also very bendy and good at pretending innocence when caught investigating off-limits places.

You can currently find Lili in the mid-South, valiantly trying to resist the lure of all the places left to explore.

Find Lili at www.lilivalente.com

CPSIA information can be obtained
at www.ICGtesting.com
Printed in the USA
FSHW020022180520
70294FS